1880: ...oud, independent Flora Lindsay find... erself not only orphaned but rich. She ... sure of two things—she will not be w... ...ed for her fortune and she must visit ...e island of Bella Careena which has f... cinated her since she found some hidde... drawings of her father's. But when she a... ives at the island she realises that benea... the loveliness run dark and deep curren... . Is the island cursed as the legends claim? Bella Careena is a Paradise, but who is the serpent in this Garden of Eden? And who is the man to whom Flora will give her heart?

ENCHANTED ISLAND

Enchanted Island

by

Linden Howard

Dales Large Print Books
Long Preston, North Yorkshire, England.

British Library Cataloguing in Publication Data.

Howard, Linden
 Enchanted island.

 A catalogue record for this book is
 available from the British Library

 ISBN 1-85389-690-X pbk

First published in Great Britain by The Hamlyn Publishing
Group Ltd., 1982

Published in Large Print 1997 by arrangement with Rupert
Crew Limited.

Dales Large Print is an imprint of
Library Magna Books Ltd.
Printed and bound in Great Britain by
T.J. International Ltd., Cornwall, PL28 8RW.

Prologue

The sky seemed to have been bleached of colour by the merciless sun; the sea that moved sluggishly against the Dorset coast was heavy and oily-looking; and still the sun climbed higher until the whole world seemed to stop breathing, its life sucked up into the great furnace that was being stoked in the sky.

In the little fishing village quaintly named 'Easter', nets were spread to dry, boats lolled on the beach, stranded by an ebbing tide, and the only refreshment came from the pungent smell of seaweed drying at highwater mark. The doors and windows of the white-walled cottages lining the main street had been flung open, as though the occupants were hopeful of catching a cupful of air. An old woman dozed uncomfortably on a stool in an open doorway, legs wide apart, serge skirts turned up unashamedly above her knees.

Lavinia Jessel, coming down the steep street to the quay with her two charges,

9

hastily averted her eyes from the immodesty of the upturned skirt and tried to divert their attention; but Edith, of course, knew exactly what was in Lavinia's mind.

'Look at that dreadful woman!' she cried shrilly.

'Hush!' Lavinia said fiercely, glaring at Edith.

'Why? She *is* dreadful to show her legs like that!'

'Be quiet, Edith,' Rose Brandon said coldly. 'Don't you know that little children should be seen and not heard?'

Rose could handle Edith as poor Vinnie never could. Rose was just sixteen, tall, well-developed, with thick, wheat-gold hair, eyes the colour of forget-me-nots, and a warm, soft mouth.

Edith glared at the older girl, pursed her small, button mouth and maintained an offended silence that did not disturb Rose in the least.

In the yard of the Fortune Inn, at the bottom of the street, a dog barked once, listlessly; beyond the Fortune was the small, private jetty where a boat waited to take Lavinia and the two girls across the three-mile strip of water to the island.

The name 'Four Winds' was written on

the prow of the boat; she was freshly painted, meticulously cared-for; to have hoisted sail would have been ridiculous on such a windless day, so the waiting crew would have to use oars; and though both were equal to the task, being large, ox-like men, the prospect of such a journey in the heat made them sullen and resentful.

Lavinia shared their resentment, not daring to voice it. The picnic had been Rose's idea, and Edith had insisted on being included, much to Rose's annoyance. It was Vinnie who carried the heavy wicker hamper; she hated being on the water, even on such a day as this. The movement of a boat made her feel sick, as Edith very well knew.

Edith Freemantle was the orphaned god-daughter of the Reverend Wilfrid Brandon, Rector of Easter and Tolfrey; she lived at the Rectory with Wilfrid, his wife Clara, and their daughter, Rose.

Edith was well-built with fine, drab hair, heavy features, and bright little eyes that regarded the world and its inhabitants with disdain; her one pleasure in life lay in finding and exposing other people's weaknesses for her own amusement.

Thankfully, Vinnie handed over the

hamper and was helped down into the boat; she sat opposite the two girls, a small upright figure, her face pink and perspiring. She was acutely uncomfortable in her heavy dress, almost suffocated by the tight bodice and high collar, her movements hampered by the drag of her very full skirts and many petticoats. The small hard bonnet fastened under her chin did nothing to shield her eyes from the glare of the sun. The girls with her wore light, muslin dresses and shady bonnets; such attire, of course, being entirely unsuitable for Vinnie, who was twenty-two, and considered herself not worth a second glance; but then, whoever gave a second glance to a governess, anyway?

The 'Four Winds' left the jetty, and two pairs of leathery, muscular arms moved rhythmically, the oars seeming to sink into the smooth sea with each thrust, then dragged clear again with such effort that sweat ran down the faces of the two men.

Vinnie felt vague pity for them, though she had little pity to spare for anyone except herself. She had been summoned to Wilfrid Brandon's study after breakfast that morning, and told that her services would not be required after the end of the month. He would see to it that she left the Rectory with a good reference; but his cousin was coming to live with them, a woman well qualified to undertake the care of young people.

Lavinia, hating him, understood; an impoverished cousin, being a member of the family, would be expected to work all hours for her bed and board, without even the meagre wages to which an outsider was entitled.

It was hardly surprising, after all, she thought bitterly; Wilfrid's meanness was a byword in the household, where his servants and womenfolk were concerned; he did not exercise such discipline towards himself—he was a man of expensive tastes.

Servants gossip; Lavinia heard bits and pieces. Wilfrid's stipend was small, but he received a very handsome allowance with which to maintain his god-daughter until she inherited a fortune on her twenty-first birthday.

So Lavinia had no heart for a picnic planned only half an hour before Wilfrid had given her notice; her head throbbed and she felt the familiar sickness churning in her stomach. No, dear God, she thought, *not* a migraine, today of *all* days!

Edith looked at her governess speculatively.

'You don't like the sea, do you, Vinnie?' she said softly. 'Are you afraid you will drown? If you DID drown, would you go right to the bottom like a stone? Right down, down, *ever* so deep? Would you, Vinnie...?'

'Please,' said Vinnie desperately, *'Please,* Edith. I have a headache...'

She should have known better, she realised; the weakness was exposed. Edith looked happy.

'Ah, poor Vinnie!' Edith crooned softly. 'Is it *very* bad? Never mind, the sea isn't rough; perhaps there *will* be a storm, though—then it will be rough going back, won't it? Will you be sick, if the boat rocks about, and the water comes in?'

The shrill voice was like a knife turning, turning, inside Vinnie's head; she closed her eyes, wishing that Rose would silence Edith with some biting reproof; but Rose hadn't heard a word of it; her eyes were fixed steadily on the long, low green mound ahead of them.

Vinnie turned her head carefully, wincing with pain. The island: Bella Careena. She

14

had been there only twice during her stay with the Brandons, and she hated the place; it was dark and secretive; a green jungle hiding a couple of crumbling old houses and a handful of derelict cottages.

It was not a large island; nearly three miles in length and two miles wide, and it lay like a curled cat contentedly sleeping in the sun.

It seemed an impossibly long journey; Vinnie sat, drenched in perspiration. She had felt unwell many times of late; but never so ill as this, so wretched that she longed to crawl away into some dark, cool place and shut out the thoughts that bedevilled her: *Where shall I go? What will become of me? How long before I find another position?*

Governesses were ten a penny in those days; Vinnie had no parents, no relatives at all except an indifferent, uninterested cousin far away in Norfolk. The future looked terrifying; she had never felt so alone, so destitute, in her life.

The boat glided to the small landing stage and was secured; shakily, Vinnie stepped ashore, faced with the task of carrying the heavy hamper once again.

For the first time, Rose seemed to be

aware that Vinnie was ill; she looked at the white, drawn face, and said quickly:

'Why don't you and Edith sit here, in the shade of the trees and rest?'

'Oh *yes!*' Vinnie agreed, with a grateful sigh.

'What are *you* going to do?' Edith asked Rose suspiciously.

'I'm going to look at the little ruined chapel,' Rose retorted.

'WHY?' Edith demanded.

'Because I want to,' Rose said sweetly; but there was a curious held-in excitement about the girl today, Lavinia thought. She was impatient to be free of them both. Vinnie had seen this excitement on one or two occasions recently; and Rose, after all, was almost a woman. Vinnie felt uneasy.

'It's too far to walk on such a hot day,' Vinnie protested.

'No it isn't, dear Vinnie! I've brought my sketch book and I intend to make some sketches of the chapel. Or a peacock, if I can find one to spread his tail for me.'

'*I* want to see the chapel! I want to come with you!' Edith cried.

'Well, you're not coming!' Rose retorted firmly. 'You'll stay here with Vinnie.'

Edith began to protest furiously; Vinnie

16

shut her eyes. If only Rose would take Edith! Then she could sit in the shade and rest, and perhaps her headache would get better. The two boatmen had gone some way along the beach on the other side of the landing stage, removed their boots and were lying on the sand, in a patch of shade cast by a tree. If they slept, Vinnie thought, she might even be able to take off her boots and stockings and cool her feet in the water. The prospect filled her with longing; but Rose, for once, was being difficult.

'Vinnie, I won't have her with me! She's a nuisance, she'll get tired and want to come back!'

'No I won't!' Edith cried angrily. 'I *won't!* I *want* to come!'

'I don't want you.' She gave Edith a none-too-gentle shove. Edith sat down abruptly on the sand and burst into tears of rage.

Rose made her escape as fast as she could; she went, fleet-footed, through the green jungle of trees, along the overgrown paths; occasionally, she heard the screech of a peacock, a sound that made her shiver deliciously. It was a weird, unearthly cry, she thought, like that of a soul in torment.

It was quite a walk to the ruined chapel—past tumbledown farm buildings on her left, then the short cut that skirted the grounds of the beautiful old house called the House of the Four Winds, its uncurtained windows like sightless eyes looking out over the English Channel.

As she approached the chapel, her heart beat fast with excitement. The excitement became almost unbearable when she heard movement ahead of her, and saw the figure step from the green tangle of bushes into a patch of sunlight.

Her body ached with longing; her feeling for him, sweet and sensuous, was a pain that seemed to pierce every part of her.

He stood smiling at her for a moment; then he put out his hands and drew her into the ruined, roofless chapel. She felt powerless to resist him. She gloried in her feeling of weakness. She was a woman! The awareness of her own body proved that fact beyond all doubt.

'I knew you would come!' he whispered.

'I thought I wouldn't be able to, after all! Vinnie's got one of her headaches and Edith wanted to come here with me...'

'Hush!' he commanded. 'Hush, Rose! There is only us two, on this island, in the whole world. We are going to make our promises to one another in this chapel, and they will be binding for ever. Say to me, "I, Rose Veronice Clara Brandon, swear to love and to cherish...till death do us part." Come on, you have to say it to me, and I have to vow to you, the words in the marriage service...please, Rose. Please.'

She looked at him, half-shocked, half-thrilled; she let her eyelids droop so that the fans of gold lashes lay against her pink cheeks.

'We can't say the marriage service,' she protested.

'Yes, we can. If we both mean it, nothing else matters. This place is our church! One day, Rose Brandon, we shall be married, properly married, and live here. We belong to one another, forever. This land will belong to me, and I shall never let you leave it!'

His determination scared and exhilarated her. He could persuade her to do things she did not want to do. He drew her close to him, making her say the words of the marriage service after him, making her look into his eyes as he spoke the words and she repeated them.

There was silence, as they finished; she

19

was trembling, frightened. Now I really *do* belong to him, forever, she thought. I have made solemn promises in a holy place.

'There!' he kissed her triumphantly. 'I wish I had a ring to give you!'

'I couldn't wear it!' she pointed out.

They walked past the chapel and sat in the shade of some trees.

'My father wants me to marry Jerome Jardine,' Rose said, leaning against his shoulder, staring dreamily up at the sky.

'You can't marry *him!* He's an old man! Besides, you belong to me. How many times must I tell you, Rose?'

They sat for a while talking, but he grew restless; he felt the stir of longing for her run like a fire through his body.

'Let's go to the cave in the bay!' he whispered yearningly. 'It's not far.'

The cave, some way down the cliffs, was reached by a path; it was dim and cool there, a perfect hideaway from prying eyes.

They lay side by side, talking for a while, his arm lying carelessly across her; but the restlessness in him would not be denied. He wanted to possess her completely, to prove to them both that she was his.

Experimentally, he ran his fingers over

her firm breasts. She tried to sit up, but he pushed her back.

'I must go, or Vinnie will come looking for me,' she whispered.

'She'll never find us here,' he murmured.

His lips moved over her forehead, her lips, her throat; one hand moved swiftly downwards to gather the flimsy skirts and petticoats together and push them determinedly up to her thighs.

'No, no!' she moaned, caught fast between terror and excitement; but in one lightning movement, he had covered her body with his, and she was conscious only of a wild singing in her ears, a furious clamour in her blood.

Vinnie looked at the little watch pinned to the bodice of her dress, and hastily began to repack the hamper that Edith had insisted upon opening.

Edith watched her sullenly, her voice hammering at Vinnie's nerves, bludgeoning them...

'Rose has been gone *ages*. I shall tell Uncle Wilfrid when we get home. I shall tell him you just sat down and did nothing, when you ought to have been looking after us. He will be angry with you...'

'I don't care!' Vinnie cried recklessly. 'I won't have to look after you much longer, anyway...thank God for that! And thank God I won't have to be near your god-father...'

'I shall tell him you swore and said awful things about him. I shall tell Aunt Clara, too,' Edith promised.

Getting unsteadily to her feet, Vinnie suddenly thought about The Reference. A slender lifeline, without which she would sink completely. Oh dear God, she will tell him, and he won't care that for months I have endured the hell of looking after this spoiled, wilful, unloveable little wretch...he will withhold The Reference...

The mists swam in front of her eyes, and she retched violently; Edith glared at her in utter disgust.

She said, wrinkling her nose: 'I shall tell them you were sick in front of me, on the sand, and you didn't *care*. Only drunk people are sick. Uncle Wilfrid said people who drink too much go to hell. I hope *you* go to hell, Vinnie. I hate you; I hope something nasty happens to you!'

If she hadn't felt so ill, Vinnie's sense of humour would have rescued her; not today, however. She staggered towards the trees and when she reached them, went forward slowly, holding on to the trunks for support.

'You've left the hamper on the beach!' Edith cried, outraged, as she ran after her.

'SHUT UP!' cried Vinnie, her nerves stretched and frayed to dangerous thinness. 'Damn you, SHUT UP!'

She was sobbing, fighting the pain in her head. She had to find Rose.

It was a long walk; eventually, she reached the chapel, Edith trailing after her, uttering shrill threats, promising vengeance, suggesting ways in which Vinnie might die, her voice like a needle that seemed to pierce Vinnie's brain, making a red mist dance in front of her eyes. There was no sign of Rose at the chapel; she hesitated and then went doggedly along the path towards the cliffs, driven by the same sixth sense that had urged her to find Rose before it was too late. Too late for what...?

Somewhere a peacock screeched, and she jumped violently. Edith ran along the path, as it came out from under some trees near the hollow, and deliberately stood in front of Vinnie, so that the governess almost fell on top of her.

Edith was singing, a horrible little song.

Plain Jane, out in the rain,
Don't let her come in again.

'That's you, Vinnie. You're a Plain Jane!'

Something snapped inside Vinnie's head; she caught the child by the shoulder, and urged her angrily along the path.

'Go!' she sobbed bitterly. 'Go. Never come near me again! *Do you hear that, Edith?* Never—come—near—me—again!'

The two people lying in the cave heard the words; the moment was spoiled. Angrily, he drew away from Rose, and she sat up, shaken, smoothing down her skirts.

The path along which Vinnie was walking led towards the top of the cliffs where low bushes grew; there was a gap in the bushes. Edith was running towards the gap, pausing every so often to turn her head, and poke out her tongue at Vinnie.

'Be careful!' Vinnie cried sharply. 'Edith, be *careful!*'

The child misunderstood Vinnie's sudden lunge in her direction, and ran faster, with Vinnie in pursuit. Suddenly, Vinnie caught the toe of her boot in a tree root and fell heavily. Her head struck the trunk of the tree as she fell forward and then, blessedly, there was no more pain, only oblivion, wrapping her in fold upon fold of silence; whilst Edith, looking back at her, decided that she was indeed drunk, and began to scramble down the path between the bushes...

'Swear it, Rose!' Wilfrid Brandon commanded fiercely. 'Swear on this bible that you will never tell another living soul what happened on the island. You have made your confession to me. That is enough. *Swear* it!'

Rose, haggard and white-faced, could only think of what she had seen: Edith, spreadeagled on the rocks at the foot of the cliffs; and Vinnie, lying on the path.

Rose began to cry; Wilfrid put his hand beneath her chin and roughly forced her face upwards until her eyes met his. His eyes were as cold as a January morning, as he held out the heavy black bible.

'I am waiting,' he told her.

'No! It is not right!'

He let go of her chin, and brought the flat of his hand in a stinging blow across her cheek; tears of pain and shame filled her eyes.

'*Why* must I swear it?' she wept.

'The answer to that is obvious. You have behaved like a common slut. You deserve a thrashing that you will never forget. No decent man would marry you, if the truth came out! *You* are going to marry Jerome Jardine!'

'I don't want to marry him!' she wept. 'I don't love him! He's *old!*'

'Love! Love!' he sneered. 'That has nothing to do with it. He will make you a good husband.'

'I won't marry him!' she said stubbornly.

The hand came relentlessly across her cheek again, making her weep afresh.

'You *will*, Rose,' he told her calmly. 'You *will* marry him. Don't tell me that you won't, because I'll not have it. As for that wretch you lay with, like a cheap little whore, you won't see *him* again. *I* shall make sure of that. Now. Take this bible in your hand and swear.'

Chapter 1

I was twenty-one years old when I first visited Bella Careena.

My parents were Mary and Richard Lindsay; my father was several years older than my mother and they were quiet people, kind and deeply affectionate towards me.

We lived in Bideford, Charles Kingsley's 'Little White Town by the Sea'; my father had a small fleet of ships, headed by the 'Devonia', that carried cargoes between Bideford, Bristol, Cardiff and other West Country ports.

Our house was a large one, high above the steep streets of the town, and the upstairs windows commanded a wonderful view of rooftops, and the wide sweep of the river Torridge, flowing away to the sea. My childhood was blissfully happy and secure; the house was always warm and full of books, and there were servants who devoted all their time and energy to our comfort and well-being.

My father was tall and good-looking; my mother had delicate colouring and masses of soft hair that always smelled of lavender and rosemary. There was a serenity about her that was very soothing; I remember her cool fingertips on my forehead, when I was ill, the tireless patience with which she amused me. When I was six years old, I had a daily governess, a woman who seemed very old to me, for she was well past middle-age; but she was an excellent teacher and her discipline was never harsh.

She died when I was eleven years old. She had no family, and my parents paid for her to be buried in the Higher Cemetery, with a headstone. It was quite unheard-of for well-to-do people to show such consideration to those who served them, but my mother said:

'She served us faithfully, it is no more than she deserves.'

One day a letter came for my mother. It seemed to distress her, and I know that my father tried to console her. She would not tell me anything about the letter, but some days later, my father did not go to his office: instead, he took me for a drive to Instow, where I watched a Punch and

Judy show on the sands, and had tea with him in a quiet little tea-room. Then he took his watch from his pocket, studied it gravely, and said that it was time for us to return home.

I was worried about my mother, and told him so; he patted my knee, and said there was nothing to worry about. Sure enough, when we returned, she came to greet us with a smile, and seemed to be her usual calm self.

I remember the time when I was twelve, and growing up, and my mother talked to me of life, and love.

'Never be led away by passion, Flora,' she said to me earnestly. 'For passion is a thing of the flesh only, and does not last; true love is not just a thing of the flesh, but embraces the spirit as well as the heart. I love your father dearly; as he loves me. Devotion to one another is the only true love, my child. Never forget that.'

The letters came twice between my twelfth and thirteenth year. Each time, the ritual was the same: a few days afterwards, my father would take me away from the house for the day, and my mother would seem happy when we returned. No amount of questioning from me was ever of the slightest use; they both fended my questions off very firmly.

When I was fourteen, my mother died very suddenly, following a stroke. I was shocked and utterly inconsolable for a long time; but youth is resilient—and at fourteen years old, I had to take over the reins of the household, manage the servants, and care for my father.

After my mother's death, my father spent more time with his books, and began to sell off his ships, one by one.

'I have no son to carry on with the business,' he pointed out to me on my sixteenth birthday, and when he saw my eyes fill with tears he put an arm around my shoulders, and said contritely:

'My dearest Flora, I did not mean to hurt you. You have brought your mother and myself great happiness.'

'Nevertheless, if I had been a boy, I could have been of help to you; I would have inherited the business, Papa. Could not a woman do so?'

'A woman—running a business? No, my love—you manage my home with a competence that would have earned your dear mother's blessing, and that is all I ask. When I am gone, you will be well provided for; then you must beware of young men who will come courting you for your money.'

'Well, they will scarcely court me for my looks,' I replied, rather bitterly.

'Do not yearn for a pretty face, Flora,' he admonished gently. 'Rather ask for qualities of the mind and heart, for such are more enduring.'

The year I was seventeen, I was spring-cleaning my father's study, with the help of one of the maids, when I came upon a sketch book.

It was my father's; he had been a talented amateur artist, as many of the pictures on our walls bore testimony, though in his later years he had put away his brushes.

The sketchbook was full of drawings, in pencil; of trees, some of them twisted into strange shapes; of ferns and foliage and flowers, and peacocks with spread tails; of an old house and a ruined chapel.

The drawings fascinated me. One each page, in the right-hand corner, was my father's signature, the date '1855' and the words 'Bella Careena'.

Bella Careena. I whispered them over and over to myself and shivered, as though

31

a cold wind had blown through the room.

At dinner that evening, I asked:

'Where is Bella Careena, Papa?'

'Why do you ask, Flora?' he demanded sharply.

I told him about the sketchbook I had found.

'Where is the sketchbook now?' he asked.

'I put it on your desk, Papa; it was wedged down behind some books on the shelves, and I thought...perhaps...you had forgotten it was there...'

My voice trailed away; I did not know what to think. I remembered the questions he had adroitly sidestepped, in my younger days—and I realised, for the first time, that the letters had ceased to come, now that my mother was dead.

I took a deep breath.

'Where *is* Bella Careena, *please*, Papa?'

'It is an island,' he said flatly. 'A small, rather insignificant one.'

'Where?'

'Off the Dorset coast,' he replied reluctantly.

'The sketches that you made were—exciting,' I said.

'Exciting? What a strange word, Flora!

They were perfectly ordinary drawings.'
His voice had an unfamiliar sharpness, for
the second time that evening.

'Did you go there often, Papa?'

'No. Only a few times,' he said
guardedly.

'It was before you married Mama?'

'Yes; really, Flora, you ask a great many
questions. It was a place with a great
variety of plant and bird life; you are
well aware of my interest in such things.
It is only natural that I should have made
sketches.'

His attitude intrigued me as I could
see that he did not wish to discuss Bella
Careena.

'You never spoke of the place, Papa.'

'What was there to say? I visited the
place on a few occasions, made some
sketches of it, and never returned to it
again. You are making a great mystery
out of nothing,' he replied.

He would not discuss it further; but the
name 'Bella Careena' had fastened small
tentacles around my imagination and they
would not be prised free.

It took me a long time to find a map
of Dorset. I had to search for it when
father was away from home, and he spent

more time in his study than anywhere else. However, eventually I found the detailed map that I wanted, and, sure enough, there was the island, about three miles from the coast. It reminded me vaguely of a cat curled asleep, tail folded around its paws.

I put the map back in its place, and said nothing to my father; next, I began to search for books that would tell me about the island. After a long search, I found one; it proved to be a treasure-house of information.

The place was rich in legend. In the old days, it had been a favourite hiding place for pirates, smugglers, men wanted for various crimes; it was suggested that secret black magic rites had been practised there by one of its owners; it had once been the refuge of a woman whose love had deserted her; the home of a witch who had cursed the island when the owner turned her adrift from it in a leaking boat; witches could not be drowned, it was said. There was no record as to whether this particular one had drowned or not.

The tentacles began to fasten themselves even more firmly on my imagination...

34

I wanted to visit Bella Careena, and I dared not ask...

But the year I was eighteen I did dare. My father said shortly:

'The island is privately owned, my dear. No one just *goes* there.'

'Yet you did.' I pointed out.

'Many years ago. By invitation.'

'Whose, Papa?'

'A friend of mine. I have since lost touch with him.' His face wore its most remote look.

The following year my father invited a young man called Alexander Arkwright to dine with us one evening. Mr Arkwright was in his late twenties, pleasant, personable, and an excellent conversationalist; he had recently joined his father in partnership as a solicitor. Mr Arkwright, Senior, had looked after my father's affairs for many years, and planned to retire in a year or two.

After dinner, he and my father spent a long time in the study. When I went to bed that evening, I took a despairing look at myself in the mirror.

I was frankly plain. As a child I had been gawky. As a woman, I was tall and big-boned. My hair, fine and fair when I

35

was young, had darkened as I grew older and was an unbecoming shade of mid-brown. My eyes were blue, my brows and nose too well-defined for prettiness. I had a stubborn chin, my mouth was too large, even my skin, instead of being becomingly pale, had a healthy glow more suited to a fisherman than a refined young lady.

Mr Arkwright came to dinner several times during the months that followed. One Sunday afternoon, he accompanied my father and myself on a short drive. A few days later, my father looked at me thoughtfully, and said, with a sigh:

'What is to become of you, Flora? I shall not always be here to protect you from the world.'

I did not want to be protected; I wanted freedom. I wanted to have wings, spread them, fly. To faraway places. To Bella Careena. I knew I would never rest until I had seen the place.

He stirred restlessly in his chair. 'You are almost twenty. Most young women are married at your age. Do you want to be an old maid?'

'*Yes!*' I cried defiantly; defiance was the only way I knew of hiding my shame at my lack of looks and suitors.

My father did not mention the matter again, until a few days before my twentieth birthday; then he reminded me that Mr Arkwright was a sober, industrious and trustworthy young man.

'I do not want a husband, Papa,' I said flatly.

'My dear Flora, you have become so pert and sharp, that you are already an old maid,' he said ruefully. 'You could fare worse than to marry a man who has such a grasp of financial affairs.'

But he never mentioned Mr Arkwright again, and the visits became more infrequent.

Every week, I took flowers to the grave of my mother and my governess. Sometimes my father accompanied me. The week before my twenty-first birthday, on a wild and windy October day, my father stood bareheaded beside my mother's grave, and I saw how he shivered.

'You should not be out on such a day,' I scolded gently. 'You already have a cold. Come along home, Papa.'

It was the last time he ever went out. The cold turned to a pneumonia that he had not the strength to fight. My twenty-first birthday passed unnoticed. My father died a few days later, and I wept bitterly for him. I felt alone and desolate.

The funeral was over; the servants had assembled to hear the will solemnly read by Mr Arkwright. The bequests my father had made to them were handsome. The amount of money he had left took me completely by surprise. We had lived comfortably, but never luxuriously; it had never occurred to me that he was a wealthy man.

He had sold his ships, and his property, and the money had been cleverly invested; after payment of bequests, the residue was left entirely to me, in trust until my twenty-fifth birthday.

'Your father feared that you would become the prey of fortune hunters,' Mr Arkwright explained, looking down his long, aristocratic nose at the papers on his desk.

'A fate I don't propose to meet,' I retorted. 'As I am unlikely to be married for my looks, I shall doubtless remain an old maid. I am fortunate enough to have money to spend as I please, and shall not need to work.'

The corners of his mouth twitched.

'You are a very outspoken young woman, Miss Lindsay,' he murmured.

'Because I do not have to make pretty speeches to win a husband,' I replied tartly. 'Well—so my father makes it a condition that I do not inherit until I am twenty-five?'

'Yes. In the meantime, you are to receive a substantial allowance that will permit you to maintain yourself in a manner in keeping with your position. Your father has appointed me as trustee of his will. If I may suggest such a thing, it might be of benefit to you to take a holiday.'

'A holiday?' I said. 'Yes. I will think it over.'

Sorting through my father's belongings, it struck me for the first time how little I knew about my parents. My father's parents had come from Hartland; my father had been their only child, having one cousin, living in Barnstaple, and who was long since dead.

I realised that I knew even less about my mother. I knew that her childhood had been happy, and that her father had been the rector of a village on the borders of Dorset and Wiltshire. She, too, was an only child and her parents died within weeks of one another when she was in her teens, she said; and then she had gone to Bristol, where she met and married my father. I could not find her birth certificate, nor my parents' marriage certificate, and I supposed that my father had given them into Mr Arkwright's keeping.

A forgotten childhood incident surfaced in my mind when I was busy one day; I remembered a scrap of conversation I had overheard between my mother and my father.

'Dearest Richard, you have made me deeply happy all these years, and shown me affection that many women would envy.

'You have shown *me* loyalty and deep affection, my dear Mary. Our marriage has been a mutual delight. Do you dare to tell yourself, now, that you were second-best only...?'

I did not hear the reply; now, for the first time, I wondered about the identity of the first woman in my father's life.

Two months after my father's death, I said to Mr Arkwright:

'I should like you to enquire if I may visit the island of Bella Careena.'

He looked astonished.

'I have never heard of the place!'

I told him that my father had visited there, by invitation, many years ago. He promised to make enquiries for me, and I waited, in a fever of impatience, for the days to pass.

I felt like a river that longs to meet the sea. I knew nothing of life and I was anxious to learn about it; after all, I was scarcely likely to know anything of love.

Mr Arkwright wrote to the present owner of the island—a man named Jerome Jardine—stating that I would like to visit Bella Careena.

A reply came to me, written on thick, expensive notepaper and covering four pages. It was from Mrs Rose Jardine, House of the Four Winds, Bella Careena, Dorset.

'My dear Flora,' she wrote, 'I cannot possibly call you "Miss Lindsay" for, although I have never met you, I feel I know you well. I knew your father many years ago, and am saddened to hear of his death. I know your mother died a long time ago; your father wrote and told me...'

The whole tone of Rose Jardine's letter was friendly and solicitous. Clearly, she knew nothing of my circumstances.

'...Jerome, my husband, wishes me to tell you that you are indeed welcome to visit us. I add my welcome to his. Stay with us for as long as you please. Consider this as your home. Our only son, Ruan, will be twenty-one this summer, and we are making great preparations to celebrate his coming-of-age. I would be glad of your help, and you will be companion to our daughter, Bella Careena (named, as she will tell you, after our beloved island!) I am sure that you will be *very* happy with us...'

I had not expected such a friendly reply; it delighted me.

Alexander Arkwright called to see me that morning. I was seated at my father's desk, reading the letter for the sixth time.

'Splendid!' I said happily.

'You *will* take care, won't you, Miss Lindsay? I shall await your letters most anxiously,' he said.

I travelled most of the way in a reserved first class railway carriage, to which a dining car attendant brought a tempting tray of food. But I was too excited to eat.

Mr Arkwright had made my travel

arrangements with great thoroughness. A hired coach awaited me to take me on the last stage of my journey. It was late afternoon when the driver guided the horses carefully down the steep little street to the yard of the Fortune Inn.

So this was the village of Easter, I thought, as I stepped down and looked around me with delighted eyes. I looked at the white beach, at the cliffs rising steeply on either side of the bay; and then I shaded my eyes with my hand and gazed seawards.

There it was! A dark hump on the skyline; the curled cat sleeping in the afternoon sun! *Bella Careena.* Still, for a few hours, tantalisingly out of reach, for I would not be making the crossing until the following day.

'It will be a fine day for the crossing tomorrow,' said a man's deep voice from behind me.

I turned slowly.

The stranger was bareheaded and wore a cloak—which was very old-fashioned, and entirely unsuited to the heat of the day; yet he looked right in it, somehow, for he was tall and lean; his face was not conventionally good-looking; two grooves ran from his nose to the corners of his long mouth, and there were small, fine lines around his dark, deepset eyes.

They were eyes one would not easily forget; brown and very alert beneath heavy black brows. He had a straight nose, and a defiant chin. Though he was considerably older than me, it was impossible to tell his exact age, for there were flecks of grey in the thick, springy dark hair that was one of his chief attractions.

When he smiled, I saw how white and even his teeth were; he inclined his head and his eyes measured me from head to toe. I felt acutely conscious of my drab mourning clothes—black has never suited me.

'If you are prone to seasickness,' the stranger said, 'you need have no fears.'

'How do you know I am going to the island tomorrow?' I challenged.

'You were looking at it as though you had never seen it before; as though the prospect of exploring it gave you considerable pleasure.'

'How very perceptive of you,' I said coolly.

'I, too, am travelling to the island,' he said. 'My name is Edwin Trehearne.

I am going to spend the summer on there.'

'I am Flora Lindsay,' I said abruptly, extending my hand.

To my discomfiture and annoyance, he did not shake hands or bow; he took my hand in his, lifted it to his lips and kissed the gloved finger-tips. It was a very theatrical gesture and I immediately distrusted him.

'Enchanté, Miss Lindsay,' he murmured.

'Are you French?' I asked.

'My grandmother fled the horrors of the Revolution—bringing her jewellery with her, which was most sensible of her!' His voice was dry and mocking. 'My mother died when I was a baby, so Grandmère Juvenal supervised my education for some years and taught me excellent French. My father was a Cornishman, as you will guess from my name.'

At that point the innkeeper's wife came forward to greet me, much to my relief. I was well aware of Edwin Trehearne's glance following me, as I entered the inn.

I was given a bedroom under the eaves. The room was at the front and faced seawards, so I could lie in bed and look at the island.

I washed, changed into a cooler dress, took the pins from my hair and brushed it. My hair was so long, it came down to my waist, and it was very thick; as I pulled the brush through it, I leaned on the broad windowsill, and pushed open the casement window; the afternoon was very still. The boats rode lazily at anchor, as though rocking themselves to sleep on the tiny waves. The tide was coming in fast, covering the sands. In the distance, the island tantalised, beckoned; lured me like a golden-haired mermaid sunning herself on a rock.

I had never considered myself imaginative; but, dreaming on a summer afternoon, I relaxed my hold on the silver-backed hairbrush, so that it fell with a clatter down to the courtyard, right at the feet of the man standing there.

Horrified, I leaned over the sill, my hair swinging down over my shoulders. He bent and picked up the hairbrush, looked up, and smiled delightedly.

'The princess in the tower!' he cried. 'Shall I return your hairbrush, my lady? Or may I have it as a keepsake?'

'It was an accident!' I cried.

He grinned wickedly. 'You look very attractive with your hair down,' he called up softly.

His words carried clearly on the still afternoon air; I had no intention of responding to his ready impudence. I drew in my head and slammed the window shut, cheeks flaming.

A few moments later, there was a knock upon the door; a maid entered, carrying my hairbrush, with its initials on the back: F.P.L.

Her face was solemn; she was about fifteen, plump and freckled.

'With Mr Trehearne's compliments, ma'am,' she said.

The private dining-room at the Fortune was furnished with mahogany, horsehair-seated chairs and a table with a starched white cloth. I didn't have the room entirely to myself, however; the table was laid for two. Mr Trehearne joined me, handsome and dignified in formal clothes.

'It seems we are dinner companions, Miss Lindsay,' he said courteously.

'I understood that this was a private dining-room,' I replied crisply.

'A private dining-room, used by over-night guests who will be going to the island,' Edwin Trehearne replied. 'This inn is owned by the Jardines. The entire village belongs to them; *and* much of the land around it. I trust your hairbrush was safely returned, Miss Lindsay?'

'Yes, thank you, Mr Trehearne,' I replied.

'I am curious as to the initial "P" on your hairbrush. I have been speculating: Penelope, Persephone. Pandora—as you see, I have a taste for Greek Mythology. Primrose—no, that would not suit you at all!'

His smile was teasing and quizzical.

'I have no intention of telling you, Mr Trehearne,' I replied primly.

He laughed; it was a rich, full sound. All my instincts sent back warning signals to my brain. Don't trust this man. He will coax your thoughts from you, and give nothing in return.

'I know more of you than you think, Miss Lindsay, though we have not met before. Your father and mine were friends, long ago,' he said calmly.

'When?' I asked, surprised.

'They met when they were at university.'

'My father has never mentioned anyone of the name of Trehearne,' I said, frowning.

'My father,' said Edwin Trehearne, 'was Sir Marcus Trehearne.'

'Was?'

'He died some years ago,' Edwin told me. 'The friendship between your father and mine ended when they both courted the same young woman; alas, she turned down your father in favour of mine and your father was extremely upset. Your father, like mine, was a proud and stubborn man, so they never patched up the quarrel; no doubt that is why he didn't mention the name of Trehearne to you.'

'What happened to the lady in question?'

'She became the second Lady Trehearne, my stepmother.'

'How do you know I am Richard Lindsay's daughter?' I asked suspiciously.

'It seemed likely that you were, when you introduced yourself. You are going to the island. Your father was there, with mine, years ago. I knew that your father had subsequently married and gone to live in the West Country, and the innkeeper's wife told me you were coming from Bideford. Simple powers of deduction, no more!'

49

I looked into the teasing eyes, and told him:

'It was because I found some sketches of Bella Careena, done by my father, that I wanted to see the place.'

'I must be honest,' Edwin Trehearne said charmingly. 'Mrs Jardine wrote me that you were coming to Bella Careena, which made it even easier to guess your identity. She tells me you are to be her secretary and a companion to Bella Careena. You will find her a very generous and understanding employer, I'm sure.'

'Employer?' I stammered.

'Yes. She has told me that your father's death makes it necessary for you to find employment.'

Astounded, I struggled to hide my feelings. Alexander Arkwright had written a formal letter—a copy of which he had given me—informing the Jardines of my father's death, and saying that I would like to visit the island. Why should they have assumed I was penniless, I wondered?

I opened my mouth to correct the mistake and changed my mind. I was an heiress, a plain young woman of twenty-one. It was an unfortunate combination.

I had thought life was dull. I wanted

adventure; I was the river hurrying to meet the sea. Let them all think, then, that I needed to work for a living.

With relief, I saw that the meal was about to be served.

However, it was almost dawn before I slept. At half-past seven, a maidservant in crisp print brought me tea and a jug of hot water. I washed and dressed and pinned up my hair with hands that shook, reminding myself that I would have to behave like a paid companion, not like Miss Flora Lindsay of Lakemba, Bideford, Devon, heiress to a fortune.

When I went down to breakfast, Mr Trehearne had already eaten his meal. I glanced out of the window, and saw him standing on the quay, looking at the island, hands clasped behind his back.

After breakfast, my luggage was brought downstairs; as I was going to the island to stay with the Jardines, I was not expected to pay for my night's stay. I looked at the little maidservant, waiting expectantly in the dining-room, and tipped her lavishly. The smile on her face made me realise for the first time the pleasures of having money to give away.

'Have you ever been to the island?' I asked.

'No, miss,' she said. 'Some of the girls from the village work there. I wouldn't care for it. I'd be feeling I was cut right off from everyone.'

The shirt-sleeved handyman carried my luggage to the private jetty, and then took Edwin Trehearne's valises, ready to be loaded.

'Good morning, Miss Lindsay,' Edwin said, strolling up to join me. 'You look excited and just a little apprehensive.'

'I feel as though I am about to embark for the other side of the world rather than cross three miles of water,' I replied.

He looked at me almost sombrely.

'In a sense you are right; to go to Bella Careena is to voyage around the world.'

He took his watch carefully from his pocket, consulted it, and remarked that it was nine-forty precisely. Then he lifted his arms and pointed ahead.

'Look!' he said. 'The boat is coming!'

It was a trim little craft, cutting cleanly through the water, making arrowheads on the flat surface, and sending out ripples on either side.

The boat was painted white and blue,

with a polished brass rail running around the small deck; I saw a man in a blue and white jersey, in the wheelhouse; another man, dark and swarthy, similarly dressed, balanced himself expertly on the prow, a circle of coiled rope in his hands. He spun it neatly as the boat came alongside and the rope made a noose over the iron bollard on the jetty. Then he jumped ashore and saluted us both.

I looked at the name, written on the prow of the boat: 'Four Winds.' I shivered as though a snowflake had brushed my cheek.

The luggage was loaded; but as Mr Trehearne turned to give me his arm and escort me on board, we heard a sudden, tremendous clatter of hooves behind us.

A closed carriage was coming at some speed down the steep little street; I held my breath, fearful of an accident, but the driver was remarkably skilled; he guided the horses expertly, checking them sufficiently to allow them to turn, and then slowing them to a more sedate trot at exactly the right moment, so that they halted only a few yards from us; their eyes were wild, their manes tossing, and they were coal-black horses such as the devil himself might have driven.

The door of the coach opened; out stepped a small, stout man, perspiring freely; by his attire, he was obviously the coachman. The man who had driven the horses so recklessly, jumped lightly from the box, put his hands in his pocket and tossed a purse full of money to the trembling coachman.

'Come, man, it wasn't such a rough ride, was it? I got us here safely—and just in time for me to join my fellow passengers!' he cried.

The coachman handed out the valise; I took a long look at the man striding with such careless grace, towards us.

He was a man to fire one's blood, I thought.

Chapter 2

He was a tall, muscular-looking man, with the powerful litheness of a tiger. He was also extremely handsome, possessing the classic good looks found on the heads of old Greek coins. His eyes were tawny, and his hair was the same colour, worn in tight little curls over his head which was most unusual; there was an air of worldliness about him that greatly impressed me.

His voice was clear and commanding; he bowed to me, smiled at Edwin.

'Good morning, Edwin; are you, too, bound for a long holiday with Rose and Jerome?'

'Yes,' said Edwin crisply. 'Damien, this is Miss Flora Lindsay, Richard Lindsay's daughter; she is going to be Rose's secretary. Miss Lindsay, this is Damien Ashley, cousin to Jerome Jardine.'

'How do you do, Miss Lindsay?' His smile was amused. 'So Rose is to have a secretary?'

'To help with her preparations for her

son's coming of age,' I murmured. 'I am also to be a companion to Bella.'

'Ah, of course.' He nodded. 'I knew your father, Miss Lindsay.'

'You, too?' I replied, astonished. 'Mr Trehearne also knew him!'

'Edwin and I spent many holidays on Easter when we were boys, and frequently visited the island,' Damien explained. 'It belonged to Jerome; my father had sold it to him. I remember that your father and Edwin's had quarrelled over a lady, and were most perturbed to find themselves staying in the same village!' He laughed, showing white teeth. 'Well, it was all a long time ago; so this is your first visit?'

'Yes,' I said.

I glanced at Edwin. His expression was aloof; he seemed to have withdrawn into himself since the arrival of Damien. That was not surprising. Damien Ashley was a man who would tower over all other men, I realised.

The boat arrowed through the smooth water, leaving a foamy wake, and I watched the coast recede; the island that had been a green hump began to take shape and form before my eager eyes. As we drew nearer, I had the impression of a great

56

many trees everywhere, of white sand, a row of cottages along the shore beside the jetty we were approaching.

Edwin pointed to the cottages, and said:

'The people who live there maintain the island, and look after Mrs Jardine and her husband.'

'It seems a very self-contained community,' I said.

'It has to be,' Damien said solemnly. 'It is a kingdom on its own, a law unto itself.'

'Nonsense!' Edwin replied sharply. 'It is subject to the same laws that govern the rest of us!'

As we approached the jetty, I saw a break in the trees; in the distance there was something that looked like a tower, and a brief glimpse of a grey church.

We drew in to a small stone jetty, identical to the one we had recently left. Edwin and Damien helped me ashore; and so I first set foot on Bella Careena.

It seemed a very silent place; the trees crowded everywhere, in a dense mass of green; at least they would give coolness and shade, I reflected.

Two conveyances waited for us, on the

57

broad path leading from the jetty; one was an open carriage, the other a trap to take our luggage. A uniformed servant helped me into the first coach, and the two men followed. When we were seated, the servant handed me a parasol, pink and pretty.

'The sun is quite fierce, ma'am,' he assured me.

As we waited for the driver to climb on to his box, I heard a strange sound; a soft tinkling of bells from the dense shelter of the trees beside the path. I listened, and it came again; a soft musical clash. I could have sworn I saw a flash of red under the trees. Then it was gone.

'That is probably Bella,' Edwin said, with a dry smile.

'What is she doing?' I asked, with a frown. 'Hiding from us?'

'Sizing us up, no doubt, before she makes herself known to us,' Damien replied.

The coachman flicked his whip, and the horses moved slowly forward.

I really did not need to use the pretty parasol, once we had turned from the jetty under the green arch of leaves that met overhead; they formed such a dense canopy that I was momentarily chilled; it was like driving through a tunnel with a circle of light at its far end. I wondered if the trees had ever been pruned.

The horses' hooves made no sound as they carried us along; there was only the faint creaking of the harness, and beyond that, a silence so still, so absolute, that I felt my heartbeat quicken; and then I heard the sound again, close beside us—the soft clash of bells, a movement, as twigs and leaves were brushed aside for someone to look at us.

I was annoyed, and turned my head sharply in the direction of the sound, but I saw nothing. Bella Careena was evidently amusing herself by keeping pace with the slow-moving coach and teasing us with the ghostly sound of bells.

The circle of light grew larger, much to my relief; the sun began to penetrate the thick screen, dappling the path with coins of gold, until we emerged into the full light of day.

As the path wound through a small clearing, I suddenly beheld a magnificent sight; a strutting peacock with its tail spread out in an exquisite fan of rich blue feathers, each with the eye clearly marked on the tail. As I leaned forward to admire it, the peacock suddenly gave a loud screech and flew up into the lower branches of the nearest tree, its beady little eyes looking down malevolently upon us.

'What a horrible sound!' I said involuntarily.

'Indeed it is,' Damien agreed. 'This is an island of peacocks. They are almost wild, and roam the place as they choose.'

We crossed the clearing, and reached a point where the path branched away to left and right, like two prongs of the letter 'Y'. The horses turned along the left-hand path.

I was facing the way we were going, and I sat forward eagerly. Again the path curved to the left and made a wide sweep around an expanse of beautifully kept lawns.

'You should close your eyes until the carriage reaches the house,' Damien teased. 'Then you will see it, as it should be seen, in all its glory. Really, the only way to approach the house is from the sea.'

I closed my eyes, as the coach turned leftwards, making a wide arc, and finally coming to rest in front of the House of the Four Winds.

'Open your eyes, Miss Lindsay!' Damien said gaily.

I opened them. I shall never forget my first sight of the house that faced south, its wide green lawns sloping down to the path where the horses stood. A long staircase of shallow stone steps led from the front of the house to this path, and the horses, from long practice, no doubt, had halted exactly at the last step.

It was more like a small castle than a house. A large, splendid building of old grey stone, with a crenellated roof, and round towers at each end. Against the many windows of its long facade, scarves of ivy lay carelessly, as though they had been blown there by the wind. At the top of the gentle flight of steps was a broad terrace, with a stone balustrade, and great stone urns were placed along the terrace at intervals, each urn foaming over with brilliant fuschia tassels. In the centre of the terrace, a door was being slowly opened, and two figures stepped out; a tall, grey-haired man and a younger woman. They did not come down the steps, but waited at the top for us, and I thought suddenly: they are like royalty, waiting to receive their guests.

'Well?' said Damien softly.

'It is so *beautiful!*' I whispered. 'This is another world.'

The steps were wide enough for three of us to walk abreast, and so we made our way upwards towards the couple waiting on the terrace.

Even on such a hot day, there was no great effort involved in mounting the steps to the terrace, so shallowly were they cut; as we neared the top, another figure stepped from the French doors that took the place of windows on the ground floor, crossed the terrace, and stood beside the waiting couple.

He was a boy of about twenty, tall, good-looking, with thick gold hair. He was taller than the other two beside whom he stood, and he held himself proudly.

'Ruan has grown into a handsome young man,' Damien said, with satisfaction. 'No doubt he is looking forward to his coming-of-age, and all the celebrations that will attend it.'

As we reached the terrace, the woman suddenly left her husband's side, and came forward, hands outstretched, as though the desire to welcome us had won the battle over dignity.

It was towards *me* that she looked; it was to *me* that she came, and to my astonishment she seized my hands, so that I dropped the parasol, letting it fall with a clatter on the top step. There were tears in her eyes; her voice was deep and husky. Her soft lips brushed my cheek.

'My dearest child!' she whispered, 'Welcome to Bella Careena! I am so happy that you are here!'

I was astonished at the warmth of her greeting towards a young woman whom she did not know, and whom she believed to be near-penniless and in search of employment. She must have been very fond of my father, I thought.

Rose Jardine was the most beautiful woman I had ever seen; she was tall and well built, with a full bust, narrow waist, and curving hips. Her hair, thick and deep golden in colour, like ripe corn, was elaborately dressed high above her face. She did not have the fashionable lily-pale look, but the sun had touched her skin only very gently, for it was the texture of a ripe peach and faintly sunwarmed. Her mouth was soft and full and her eyes were the bluest I have ever seen. The thick lashes, the finely-arched brows, the rounded chin and the long neck had been perfectly fashioned, as though by a master craftsman. She wore a delicately tucked and ruffled dress of pink; it had frills at the neck and elbow length sleeves; the skirt was caught up into a bustle at the back. Her shoes exactly matched her dress; I saw the gleam of gold at her throat, and on her slender wrist.

It was not fair that one woman should possess so much beauty, I thought dismally; I was acutely aware of my own plainness; this woman, so softly and prettily curved, carried her height beautifully. *I* was big-boned; at the moment I felt gawky, and very dowdy, in my hot black mourning attire.

'Rose,' said Damien plaintively, 'I swear we are invisible to you. Have you no welcome for us?'

She laughed, and apologised prettily, offering each of them a soft, perfumed cheek.

'Damien, I am delighted to see you. You did not say when you could come, and I imagined Irene would be with you.'

'She will be here soon,' he told her. 'She had last-minute affairs that delayed her;

as for me, I could not wait to exchange the heat and noise of London for this Paradise!'

Rose smiled at Edwin.

'You, Edwin? Are you tired of all your responsibilities?'

'How can I be otherwise, when you offer such an attractive alternative, my dear Rose?' he said charmingly. 'Gloucestershire cannot compete with this incomparable island. Your proposition was most tempting; squander a summer here, you said. I owe myself a long holiday; and I have left a good man in charge of my affairs.'

Rose turned to me and said:

'Come, Flora; Ruan and Jerome are waiting to meet you.'

Rose was tall for a woman; Jerome was more than six feet in height, a man who dwarfed us all, broad-shouldered, upright, with rugged features, and brown eyes that were friendly, belying the severity of his mouth and cragginess of his face. His hair was silver grey, brushed high above his forehead and then falling back in deep waves. One hand rested on a silver-topped walking-stick.

I realised that he was much older than his wife; but when he smiled, his mouth lost its severity. His voice was clear and resonant.

'Welcome to Bella Careena, Miss Flora Lindsay!' he said; and, in spite of Damien's jest about 'King Jerome' I thought that Jerome Jardine had a very regal bearing at that moment.

Ruan Jardine resembled his mother more than his father. His thick, springy hair was the same golden colour, his bright hazel eyes looked at me with interest; he had his mother's well-defined features and generous mouth. I thought him a pleasant and very personable young man.

'Welcome to the island,' he said to me.

'There is one member of the family missing,' Jerome Jardine told me wryly. 'Isabella has chosen to absent herself. She prefers to see before she is seen. She has no doubt made herself well aware of your arrival and journey here.'

'Isabella?' I queried.

'She was christened Isabella Serena Catherine,' Rose told me. 'As a child she could not manage the "Isabella", so what more natural than that she should shorten it to Bella and then add "Careena" after her beloved island? You'll meet her soon enough, Flora. At this moment, I am sure

66

you need rest and some refreshment.'

She put her hand on her husband's arm; I saw the look of love and tenderness that flashed between them as they led the way into the house. We followed them, the servants bringing up the rear, with the luggage.

Other servants waited in the big cool hall, with its carved furniture, and faded old wall hangings.

Rose spoke to Damien.

'Will you stay here until Irene joins you? As you have come earlier than I anticipated, Seawinds is not quite ready for you,' she said to him.

'In that case I shall be delighted to accept your hospitality,' he told her.

She signalled to one of the servants and said that Mr Ashley would occupy the east tower suite. The suite in the west tower was to be Edwin's, I gathered.

I felt a light touch on my arm; Ruan was smiling at me.

'I think you'll be good for Bella,' he murmured.

'You make me sound like a dose of medicine!' I protested.

'I don't mean to; it's just that she hasn't any young company, except me and I have

67

been kept busy now that my father isn't in good health. She only has Nanny Radford, her old Nurse; Nanny has been with Bella ever since she was born.'

'Are you looking forward to your coming-of-age?' I asked him.

He sighed.

'I'm not sure I'll enjoy all the fuss. Still, the first of September is several weeks away yet.'

He went across to speak to one of the servants. Jerome said to me:

'I liked your father, Flora.'

I shook my head, puzzled.

'You all knew him: you—Mr Trehearne —Mr Ashley. Yet he never mentioned any of you to me.'

'It was a long time ago; twenty-five years. I didn't know him well, more's the pity. He rented a house for a couple of months, near where I was living, and it was a casual acquaintanceship, I suppose. We had a few meals together, at the Fortune, and discussed books and ships. Was his marriage to your mother a happy one?'

'Very happy,' I said.

'I'm glad to hear it,' he said.

'Did you ever meet my mother, Mr Jardine?'

68

'Jerome, my dear Flora—Jerome, not "Mr Jardine". We want you to consider yourself one of the family.'

He didn't answer my question, for Rose came over to me at that point.

'I will take you to your rooms, Flora,' she said, for all the world as though I was the most honoured guest of all.

She led me across the great hall, over grey flagstones, whose coldness was softened by several old eastern rugs; at each end of the hall, I saw twin, shallow staircases, curving upwards to a long gallery from which led many doors. We went up the stairs together.

'I thought you would prefer to be at the back of the house,' she said, opening a pair of double doors with a flourish. 'You have sea views from the front; but I think the sea looks empty and lonely. I believe you would prefer to have a view of the island.'

The room was large, airy and prettily furnished; it was a sitting-room, with comfortable chairs, a well-filled bookcase, plants, a writing-desk: a door led from it to a bedroom, with a great four-poster bed, splendidly draped in blue velvet.

The deep-set windows looked out over

treetops. I saw the tower of an old church, not far from the house; it was the one I had seen from the boat. Away westwards, towards the Devon coast, the island seemed to curve up fairly steeply. I had tantalising glimpses of sun-speckled water, and ahead of me was the mainland, a hazy purple ribbon in the distance. The view immediately below me was delightful; lawns unrolled like green velvet towards a small marble temple, with a cupid on top of the round cupola; I glimpsed the tantalising shimmer of a lake in the distance; there were massed bushes of rhododendrons, fuchsia, many plants whose names I did not know.

I looked eastwards, at the ruined tower some distance from the house; I had seen it from the boat.

'What is that?' I asked Rose, pointing.

'The Folly,' she said lightly. 'There are two such follies on the island. The other is a very delightful cottage in the grounds where Bella lives with Nanny Radford. When you and Bella have come to know one another, then perhaps you will live in the cottage with her.'

'Why does Bella live apart from you?' I asked.

'Oh, it is not apart, not in *that* sense! I love my daughter dearly; her affection for me has never been in doubt! It is simply that she is a strange child, coming now to womanhood, and wanted to have, as she put it, "a little house of her own, amongst the trees." This island is a strange place, you will find; haunted, some say. It casts its own spells, and they are very potent. I want *you* to love it, also. I want you to stay. It is *right* that you should be here!'

'Why?' I asked, still nonplussed.

'Oh, Flora, dear child!' She caught hold of my arm and looked almost pleadingly into my face. 'Don't vex yourself with questions. *I* want you to be here. Let that suffice.'

'Did *you* know my father?' I asked.

'Yes. The year I was sixteen. Afterwards, when he married and moved away, we lost touch.'

I said, with some exasperation:

'Whenever I seek to know more about my parents, I find closed doors.'

'Perhaps one should not look for keys to every door, Flora.'

'It is natural to be curious concerning one's parents.'

'Whatever it is you wish to know, *I*

71

cannot tell you,' she answered. 'Do you have happy memories of them?'

'Yes. Very happy ones.'

'Then you are lucky. My father was hard and unloving; he punished me severely for the smallest misdemeanour. My mother suffered from a number of ailments: fatigue, migraine, "turns"—all of which seemed to necessitate her spending most of her time in a darkened room. The years I have spent with Jerome have been very happy. Nothing changes here. I don't like change.'

'I would have thought it was inevitable in life,' I pointed out.

'Oh, Flora, how old and wise you sound. Like—' she stopped abruptly.

'Like whom?' I pressed.

'Vinnie,' she said. 'She was my governess. Well, now, Flora, this is to be your home for as long as you wish. You must not look upon Jerome or myself as your employers. You are one of us.'

I was at Bella Careena under false pretences. Why didn't I tell the truth, then? Perhaps because I wanted to be accepted on my own merits, to prove myself capable of earning a living, even though I didn't need to do so.

She kissed my cheek, and said:

'I'll have some hot water and a cool drink sent up to you. Then you can rest until lunchtime. Did you have a comfortable night at the Fortune?'

'Oh, yes,' I told her. 'I met Mr Trehearne there.'

'His father, Sir Marcus Trehearne, designed all the gardens on the island. Jerome asked him to do so because he had laid out the grounds of his house in Gloucestershire so beautifully, and he was an authority on plants, as well as being an artist. You will enjoy seeing his workmanship; especially the Grottoes. He was a man with a vivid imagination.'

'Mr Ashley told me that *his* father once owned the island,' I said.

'Yes, it's quite true—the island belonged to Damien's father, once. He found the place an encumbrance. Jerome is a generous man, Flora; he insisted that Seawinds should be kept as a home for Damien whenever he wished to come here. It's at the other end of the island.'

She crossed the room; at the door she paused and said:

'They come every summer; Damien, and his wife, Irene.'

73

Chapter 3

I sponged away staleness and heat in silk-soft water. A maid unpacked my luggage and put away my clothes.

The room seemed suddenly airless, the silence hot and heavy. I was supposed to be in mourning for my father. Would the Jardines think it odd if I wore a light-coloured dress? Probably not; this was not Bideford, where the conventions had to be observed.

I settled for a dress of cream voile, with lavender coloured ribbons and an edging of lace at the neck and sleeves, fastened my hair behind my neck and splashed lavender water liberally on my hot forehead.

It was nearly lunch-time; I went out of the room, along the gallery to the top of the stairs and looked down.

A young girl stood in the hall, hands clasped behind her back; she was staring upwards, and her glance met mine gravely. She did not smile nor move.

I knew at once who she was.

I went slowly down the stairs, and as I reached the bottom step, she walked across to me, still clasping her hands behind her back. She looked me over from head to toe.

This tall, slim girl could have passed for sixteen. Her hair was much darker gold than her mother's; it was thick and curly, was drawn back from her face, and fastened with a large bow on the nape of her neck. Her eyes were the same brilliant blue as her mother's.

'Are you Flora Lindsay?' she asked.

'Yes,' I said.

She held out her hand.

'My name is Isabella Serena Catherine Jardine,' she told me gravely. 'I do not like the first three names at all, and the fourth is unnecessary because everyone here knows that I am the only daughter of Mr and Mrs Jardine. My real name is "Bella Careena", the same as the island. I *am* the island. I am exactly like it. Do you understand me, Miss Lindsay?'

'Not really,' I admitted frankly.

'It doesn't matter. Soon you *will* understand. I know this island better than anyone else. I shall show it all to you. We will begin this afternoon. If you are going to stay here for a time, you must know your way around.'

I looked into the blue eyes and found them cold, and I realised that Bella did not share her mother's pleasure in my arrival.

'Are you a good walker?' she demanded, in a tone of voice that said she rather doubted the fact.

'I am considered to be so,' I said mildly.

'I will lend you my parasol,' she said. 'It is made of scarlet silk, shaped like a pagoda, and has bells hanging around the edge; when the bells tinkle, the sound is very pretty.'

'Is that the sound I heard this morning?' I asked.

'No. You heard the tinkling of the bells sewn on my dress.'

I looked, with raised eyebrows, at the simple, unornamented white dress she was wearing, and she frowned impatiently.

'I wasn't wearing *this* dress. Nanny Radford is deaf and short-sighted, so I sewed bells on some of my dresses—then she could hear me and know I was safe. I put red ribbons on too, because red shows up best when people can't see. I've always done it, for her; well—I rather like it anyway. Ruan says it's childish, at my age, but I don't care what he thinks.'

'Why did you hide away from me this morning?' I asked.

'I wanted to see what you looked like,' she replied coolly.

'I trust I met with your approval!' I said tartly.

She said calmly: 'I don't need a governess, and I've never had one. Mama and Papa taught me everything. I can read, write, paint and sew, speak French and German and play the piano. I also know how to conduct myself in company, and be agreeable to people. So there is no need for you to teach me *anything*, Miss Lindsay.'

I tried to hide the twitching of my lips. 'You may call me Flora,' I said.

'Thank you. There really was no need for you to come here, you know.'

'I came at your mother's invitation; she, at least, has welcomed me,' I retorted. 'It is neither kind nor polite of you to make me feel unwelcome.'

She said calmly: 'I don't wish to make you feel unwelcome, but there is something I must tell you: I do not intend to leave this island yet, and I shall not do so until I am ready. I hope you will not try to persuade me that it is for my own good that I should leave here. I wonder why mama was so anxious to have you here? She has talked of nothing else for days. One would imagine you were the daughter of her oldest friend, yet I have never heard your name mentioned until a few weeks ago.'

I wondered if she was jealous; but the sudden arrival of Edwin put an end to further conversation, and she ran joyously to him.

'Uncle Edwin! I hope you are going to stay for a long time.'

She flung her arms round his neck, kissed him and raced upstairs; he looked quizzically at me.

'You look cool and elegant,' he told me. 'Black doesn't suit you at all.'

'I'm in mourning for my father,' I said.

'No one observes the conventions here. I am still trying to fit a name to the tantalising letter "P" on your hairbrush. So far I've made no progress. Don't tell me, or you will spoil the game!'

'It's a great deal of nonsense about nothing!' I retorted.

'Ah, I have it! *Phyllida! Pepita?* No, you do not look sultry enough for a "Pepita".

79

Ah well! It is not every man who has an acquaintance with a lady's hairbrush! It suggests all kind of scandalous liaisons!' he replied solemnly.

A latent sense of humour awoke in me, and made me laugh, unwillingly.

I saw approval in his glance.

'We *are* making progress after all,' he murmured.

'What a man of moods *you* are, Mr Trehearne!' I replied lightly. 'Early this morning, you seemed quite—sombre.'

'Perhaps because I foresaw that you were coming under a spell...'

'The spell of the island?'

'No. A spell as potent, however, and even more dangerous. I refer, of course, to Mr Damien Ashley. His reputation for spell-casting is well known.'

He went coolly on his way, leaving me furious and struggling for words.

I walked towards the open door and stood looking at the crinkled blue sea, trying to find some breath of air. There was none. The glitter of the sun on the water was fierce and unrelenting.

Ruan found me standing there, when he ran up the steps and crossed the terrace, some minutes later.

'Flora? You've met Bella?' he asked.

'Yes. Your sister wants nothing of the outside world, it seems,' I told him. 'Do you feel the same complete affinity with the island that she feels?'

'Oh, Bella is a law unto herself—like the island. She's strange. "Fey" is the word, I think. It's different for me; I have been away to school, *and* abroad. I studied Art in Italy. For such a small country, it is packed with treasures: paintings, sculpture, architecture; a feast of beauty.'

'You sound as though your heart is there still!' I teased.

'Flora—I may call you that, mayn't I?—you have guessed the truth. Bella Careena can never be *my* world!' He spoke with great passion. 'Mama says my father must not know that. It would distress him.'

'He will have to know one day; men must follow their own paths in life,' I argued.

'And women?' he asked, with a smile of gentle amusement.

'Oh, they are not so fortunate, as a rule!' I replied lightly.

There were seven of us for lunch in the

81

big, cool dining-room: Jerome and Rose, Ruan and myself, Damian, Edwin and Bella. Over lunch, Bella told her mother that she proposed to take me on a tour of the island during the afternoon. Rose shook her head.

'My darling child, it is *much* too hot for such an expedition.'

I saw the look of disappointment on Bella's face; but the greatest surprise was the look that Jerome gave his wife.

It was a look of such blinding love and tenderness that I felt I had trespassed by witnessing it; I had never before seen love between husband and wife so clearly expressed; for Rose smiled across the round table at her husband, and it was a smile that accepted and returned in full measure the great love he had for her.

'You cannot expect poor Flora to walk so many miles in this heat!' Ruan was protesting to his sister.

'*I* can do it!' Bella retorted, in genuine surprise.

'For such a delicate-looking young lady, you are as strong as a horse,' Ruan teased his sister.

'We shall *all* go,' Rose said, unexpectedly. 'Except you, Jerome. You must rest, as the doctor has ordered. We are *not* going to walk, however; we shall travel in two open carriages.'

I had no hat suitable for such an outing; well—if the conventions were unobserved here, as I had been told, it would not matter if I went hatless, I decided. A maid brought the scarlet silk parasol to me, with great ceremony, telling me that Miss Bella had sent it. It was very pretty and the bells sang softly as I moved it.

I decided to wear my gold locket; my mother had possessed little jewellery, never caring for adornments, with the exception of this gold locket set with seed pearls and hanging from a fine gold chain. Inside was the only photograph I possessed of my mother, not a very good one, for it did not do justice to her delicate colouring; but I liked the tale of the locket: when Grandfather Lindsay was courting my grandmother, who lived in Bristol, he often sent presents by boat to the Welsh Back at Bristol, instructing my grandmother to call on the Captain and collect these love tokens. The locket had been an engagement present.

I showed it to Rose, just before we left the house, and told her the tale.

'What a lovely story!' she said.

I opened the locket and showed her the photograph; she studied it intently for several seconds.

'So that is your mother, Flora?' she remarked, at last.

'Yes.'

'Did you love her very much?'

'Of course.' The question surprised me. Rose straightened, smiled, and said it was time we were leaving.

We split into two groups; Damien escorted Rose in the first carriage, with Ruan, Bella, Edwin and myself in the second one. Ruan remarked, laughingly, that as Dowte, his mother's coachman, was very deaf, his mama and Damien could talk as freely as they pleased.

The carriages took the path along which we had come that morning, until we reached the place where it joined the main path; then the horses plodded back towards the small landing stage, and, when we were halfway there, the carriages stopped.

The little bells on my parasol clashed softly together, as the four of us stepped down. Rose and Damien made no move;

Damien waved his hand languidly, and said:

'We shall sit here in this patch of shade, whilst you explore the Folly. I am in no mood for climbing steps on such a day, and neither is Rose.'

The Folly stood in a small clearing at the end of a footpath that wound under an arch of tree branches. The 'ruined' tower was of a type that had been popular in the previous century, when gardens were often most romantic affairs. There was an arched door, and two empty windows, like eye-sockets.

Ruan told me: 'The island was once jointly owned by two brothers, Charles and Barkeley Selwyn, who fell out with one another. Charles built The House of the Four Winds, on *his* part of the island, and Brother Barkeley was furious; he said it was far superior to Seawinds—which is now Damien's house—and, of course, that *is* true. So the disgruntled Barkeley built himself a tower high enough to overlook the grounds of Charles' house that he coveted so much!'

It was not a new story. I had heard versions of it before; I watched Bella Careena, running ahead, not seeming to feel the intense heat, and Edwin following her at a more leisurely pace.

'So now Mr Ashley owns Seawinds?' I said.

Ruan nodded. 'Damien's father, Sylvester Ashley, was first cousin to Jerome's father, Caspar Jardine. Sylvester was the sole owner of Bella Careena, but he couldn't be bothered with the place, and considered it a liability. My grandfather Jardine made a lot of money out of the Napoleonic Wars, you know; for men in the field of battle need provisioning and clothing and they must be well supplied with weapons. My grandfather was a shrewd man, and probably undercut his competitors for tenders to supply all the needs of the troops; he ended up with a comfortable fortune, and he wanted the island; Sylvester was only too glad to sell it to him; he preferred to spend his time in London amongst the ladies and the gambling salons and he had lost a great deal of money. I believe he drove a hard bargain with Caspar Jardine, and asked far more than Bella Careena was worth, for all the buildings had fallen into disrepair and no one was living there. It must have been a desolate place, but grandfather saw it, in his mind, as it is today: it was to be his kingdom. It seems as though there was some kind of curse on the place, though.'

A curse; it sounded interesting. I looked at him expectantly, as I furled my tinkling parasol, and bent my head to enter the low arch that led to a flight of stone steps.

The steps were only wide enough to take one person at a time, and I went ahead of Ruan. Bella's laughter floated back to me, sweet and clear, followed by the resonant sound of Edwin's voice.

'Tell me about the curse,' I said to Ruan.

'It was said that strange fertility rites were performed in a grove of trees, and black masses were held by a renegade monk who lived in the ruined chapel; they say his ghost still haunts the place.'

I paused, to look out of a narrow window; the blood was pounding in my ears, and I felt giddy; though we had not accomplished half the climb, we were both out of breath, and Ruan was glad enough to rest whilst he finished the tale.

'Grandfather Jardine brought a young bride here; they had one son, my father, who was born on the island. There was a big christening party, and a boatload of people came over from the mainland, but a storm blew up, the boat capsized, and several of them were drowned; and Grandmother Jardine died, suddenly, that same day, of a seizure. We were intruders, you see; the curse was working! Grandfather left the island in the hands of an agent and went back to live in Dorset; he was absolutely desolate at the death of my grandmother, for theirs was truly a Romeo-and-Juliet romance, I am told. Grandfather lived another thirty years, and though my father often visited the island, he never settled here; not until he married my mother. That was twenty-three years ago. He was thirty-eight then.'

I made some rapid calculations and said in astonishment:

'Then your father is now sixty-one years old!'

'Yes,' he agreed. 'Twenty years older than my mother.'

In silence, we finished the climb up the corkscrewing stairs; when I reached the top, my heart was hammering, and my legs felt like jelly.

The space on which we stood was only just wide enough to hold the four of us, and the stone parapet was barely waist high. I looked down on a green sea of treetops; I could see the girdle of bright blue water around the island, the houses by the jetty, the farmhouse on the other side of the jetty, where toy-like cows moved slowly in the heavy heat.

'Isn't it beautiful up here?' Bella Careena said happily.

'Yes,' I replied, with an effort.

Edwin looked sharply at me.

'Don't you like heights, Flora?' he asked.

'Not very much,' I admitted; it was an understatement. The ground seemed to draw me, as though urging me to lean over, too far, so that I would fall...

I battled with nausea; Edwin's voice was even sharper.

'You should not have come,' he said. 'Why didn't you say you didn't like heights?'

'To give in to one's fears is cowardice,' I told him.

Bella looked at us with interest. 'Poor Flora!' she said softly. 'It is easy to be frightened here. There are curses on this island... This is a witch-tower. Years ago, it was the home of a witch who was turned adrift in a boat...'

'It was not! Barkeley Selwyn built it,' Ruan retorted.

'Don't be frightened, Flora,' Bella Careena said softly. 'You won't fall. Look at the view; isn't it beautiful?'

'Yes,' I said briefly.

'You haven't looked properly.' She tugged at my sleeve insistently. 'Look, there's a peacock—see that flash of blue? The peacock frightened you this morning, when it screeched, didn't it? Peacocks sound almost human when they cry out.'

'For Heaven's *sake!*' Edwin rounded angrily on her, and Ruan jerked his sister's hand from my arm. The double rebuke made her eyes fill with tears, and she turned away tossing her head.

'Let's go below,' Edwin said; I heard the exasperation in his voice. I put my hand to my throat; I felt as though I was going to choke.

I was glad to reach the bottom of the tower; Edwin went in front of me, Ruan behind me, while Bella brought up the rear.

As we walked back to the carriage, Ruan and Edwin lagged behind, talking so quietly together that I could not hear their conversation. Bella walked beside me.

90

I opened the parasol, shielding my face, listening to the tinkle of the bells, a sound that suddenly seemed eerie.

'I can tell you all about the island,' Bella assured me, watching me closely. 'Ruan doesn't really know much, neither does Uncle Edwin. *I* have seen a book that tells everything.'

'Where?' I asked; and her face became secretive.

'I won't tell you. It's in a secret place. It's all true, though. About the smugglers, and the people who hid here so they wouldn't be captured and killed, and the wicked monk. It's quite creepy, you know, on stormy nights; when the wind is in the trees, it sounds like the voices of all the people who ever lived here, calling to each other.'

'Are you trying to frighten me?' I demanded.

Her eyes were guileless.

'Of *course* not, Flora! Why would I do such a thing?'

'So that I shall go away from the island, perhaps.'

'If you did so, mama would be most upset. She would be angry with me for frightening you. She says you belong here;

91

I heard her tell papa so; but you *don't* belong, Flora, you DON'T! You weren't born here, as I was. You aren't part of the island, as *I* am. Even Ruan isn't part of it, though *he* was born here. Only ME....!'

I did not know what to make of her extraordinary remarks. I was still trying to puzzle them out when we reached the carriage where Rose sat, very upright, but looking pale and fatigued. She smiled, and the smile seemed to be an effort.

'Did you enjoy the view from the top of the tower?' she asked me.

'Flora suffers from vertigo,' Edwin answered crisply.

'Do you feel quite well, dear?' Rose asked. 'Or do you wish to return to the house?'

'I'm well enough now that I'm on the ground again,' I said, trying to make light of it.

I was acutely aware of Damien's eyes upon me; tawny eyes, full of warmth; the sun, slanting through the trees, gave burnished richness to the tight curls that clustered over his head. I had never seen such a handsome man, nor one so full of vitality. There was an extraordinary magnetism about him, as though he silently drew me towards him.

My heart lurched wildly. Vainly, I tried to steady its wild beating; how fatally easy it would be to fall completely under the spell of Damien Ashley. What would it be like to be loved by him...?

I knew nothing of the love between a man and a woman. My mother had warned me never to be led away by passion, insisting that devotion between two people was the only true and lasting love. Passion brought children into the world, but it was something that only a man should feel, not a woman. Passion, in a woman, was immodest, she declared.

I thought of passion as a fever; a wild tumult, a madness of the heart, a craving for the touch, the look, the nearness, of just one person.

I pulled my thoughts back to the ground. Damien had a wife, a woman called Irene.

I gathered my trailing skirts in my hand as the coachman helped me to my seat.

We set off at a sedate pace, and when we reached the landing stage, Ruan pointed out the farm to me.

'It covers a big area, as you see,' he said. 'It supplies us with all our vegetables, eggs, milk, butter and cheese. It's managed by the Cleggs, and their two grown-up sons.'

On the right of the landing stage was another path that I had not noticed earlier that day. The carriages turned along this path, and soon we were passing the backs of a row of cottages that faced towards the mainland. Each cottage was trim and well-kept, with its own vegetable plot. Ruan explained that the cottages were occupied by retired servants, and by families of servants who still worked at the House of the Four Winds as well as at Seawinds; he was obviously proud of the fact that his father cared for his tenants and made their well-being the most important part of his administration.

'There's another cottage,' Bella Careena said importantly. 'It's on the edge of a wood, hidden by trees. Laurie Perkins lives there. He's odd, because he likes to be alone and doesn't care for people. He has a little forge where he shoes the horses. He keeps rifles clean, too, and sharpens the arrows.'

I stared at her in sudden consternation; Ruan shook his head at me, and smiled reassuringly.

'No one does any hunting here, Flora.

It's forbidden, anyway. The arrows are for sport—archery is a great favourite with mama and papa, though papa indulges less often these days. The rifles are also for use on targets and clay pigeons only!'

We left the cottages behind and the scenery became wilder and more beautiful; we passed an ornamental pool and a tiny Grecian temple standing on a rise above massed purple rhododendron bushes and wild fuschia. Looking closely about me, I realised that what appeared to be a delightful artlessness was, in reality, the result of careful planning. We rode through a grove of birches, and beyond it was a tiny rock-girdled pool with a stone figure of a girl standing in a niche above it; tasselled fuschia tumbled in a cascade around her.

I exclaimed over it with such pleasure that Ruan ordered the coachman to stop, so that I might step down and admire it more closely.

'Edwin's father designed it so,' he explained. 'An island made into a garden.'

'Not a formal garden,' Edwin told me, 'but with some parts of it left wild and unspoiled. The most interesting gardens, like the most interesting people, are constructed on that principle, wouldn't you agree, Flora?'

Bella frowned and said crossly:

'Why do you talk in riddles, Uncle Edwin?'

'My dear child, I do not talk in riddles. When you are old enough, you will discover the sense of what I say.'

'Tell Flora about the grottoes your father designed,' Bella commanded Edwin.

'She is about to see them for herself,' Edwin reminded her.

'We'll go to the Shell Grotto, up above Neptune's bay, first of all,' Bella said, with a touch of imperiousness.

'Mama does not care for that place,' Ruan pointed out.

'But we *must* go there! It's my favourite! Mama can sit in the carriage and talk to Damien.'

'Is there something sinister about this particular grotto?' I asked.

Bella shrugged; she was obviously dying to tell me the tale.

'There was an accident there, years ago, before Ruan and I were born. Mama came here for the day with her governess, Lavinia Jessel, and a little girl called Edith Freemantle, who lived with mama's parents. Edith was playing on the cliffs above the grotto—it's the only place where the cliffs are really high—when she fell over and was killed. Mama found her; she had been sitting, sketching, in the ruined chapel nearby.'

Ruan shook his head at his sister.

'Mama hates to be reminded of that time; no wonder. It must have been a great shock for her,' he pointed out.

'Where was the governess when Edith was killed?' I asked.

'She was ill, or strange in the head, or something,' Bella replied. 'Miss Jessel—Vinnie, as they called her—wasn't looking after Edith as she should have been, and it was all hushed up afterwards. She was sent away in disgrace.'

'That hardly seems fair if she wasn't responsible for her actions,' I pointed out.

Bella had already lost interest in the fate of the governess.

'There's the Grotto of the Peacocks to see,' she told me, 'that's between the church and the house; then there's the Grotto of the Four Winds, which is near the house; and, right at the other end, beyond Clegg's Farm, is mama and papa's

97

very private Sun Grotto.'

'Aren't you forgetting the fifth grotto?' Ruan teased.

'No,' said Bella shortly, as though she did not want to discuss the subject.

'Where is the fifth grotto?' I asked.

'No one knows. It has never been found,' Edwin replied calmly. 'I have spent a great deal of time searching for it. I shall search for it until I find it.'

I wanted to ask why, but Bella Careena was looking at Edwin with a curious expression on her face, and I decided to save my questions until later.

I knew that I was falling under the spell of the island; yet I had a strong feeling that there was a sinister quality that ran like a dark river beneath all its beauty and strangeness. Perhaps it was because of its history, I thought: there had been plenty of tragedy and violence here.

The ground rose gently upwards as we approached the western end of the island; we rode through leafy tunnels and under beech trees, down aisles of dark, pointed firs, through groves of slender birches, past sturdy oaks. We passed a tiny waterfall, a natural spring tumbling between rocks; and then we reached a clearing beyond which was a grassy plateau. On the plateau stood a white house facing the mainland.

'That's Seawinds,' Bella told me.

It was not so large nor so grand as the House of the Four Winds, but it looked very gracious, with a terrace all around it, and stone urns at each corner, filled with scarlet geraniums.

I looked at it, and thought of Damien living there with Irene; my heart felt like lead.

The island was criss-crossed with small paths, apart from the main paths which were like roads, well-made, able to take the coaches without difficulty.

'I know every path on the island,' Bella told me proudly.

Everywhere, we came upon peacocks, flashes of blue-green amongst the trees; arrogant birds, with an unearthly sound to their screeching, their bright little eyes proclaiming us intruders in their domain. Away to the left, half-hidden by trees, I saw the ruined chapel.

'That's where the monk lived,' Bella said, her eyes never leaving my face. 'He was terribly wicked; not like a *proper* monk. He offered up human sacrifices; at night, he still walks about the island...'

'Don't talk such utter rubbish!' Ruan said curtly. 'What are you trying to do—frighten Flora? Drive her away?'

She didn't answer him; she sat with downcast eyes until we had travelled a short way along a path that seemed to end in cliffs. We came to a group of trees, and there, in the shade, was the coach containing Rose and Damien. Our coach pulled in behind the first one, and we all got out.

'We're going to look at the Shell Grotto,' Bella told her mother.

'I shall not come with you,' Rose said quietly. 'Do be careful, all of you.'

'The path isn't dangerous, Mama,' Ruan told her gently. 'It's steep, in places, and we have to watch our step, that's all. Edwin and I will take care of the girls.'

'I am going to return to the house,' she told us. 'The heat has given me a headache.' She gave Damien a small, strained smile. 'There's really no need for you to accompany me, Damien; Dowte can take me back.'

Dowte turned the horses and set off for the House of the Four Winds. The rest of us went to the cliff top, and I saw the path—steep, stony, but—as Ruan had said—not dangerous if one was reasonably sure-footed. It was a fair drop to the beach, and a spine of rocks poked through the sand of the secluded little bay.

Ruan and Edwin went first, then Bella and I followed, with Damien bringing up the rear. Some way down the path, I saw a cave, with a broad, rocky ledge in front of it. It was easy enough to step from the path to the ledge; the path went on, past the opening, right down to the beach.

'This way,' Ruan said, holding out his hand.

I stepped into the cave, my heart beating fast.

'Well?' said Damien softly.

I instantly hated the place; unreasonably, for it had been marvellously adapted to make a natural grotto; a pattern of shells, stones and sea-smoothed glass had been inset into the walls to make a mosaic. Stones and shells had been carefully and painstakingly matched; the result was a picture of a sea-serpent, with a mermaid riding on his back; the eyes of the serpent and of the mermaid had been made of pieces of glass that glittered in the sun.

'It looks beautiful by moonlight,' Bella Careena whispered. 'Then the eyes glitter, the moon sparkles on the sea and the ghost of poor little Edith walks along the beach.'

'You're frightening Flora again,' Ruan said angrily. 'You're obsessed with ghosts and legends and all the silly gossip about this island.'

She looked angrily at him.

'Gossip? You forget that this is where Edith died!' she cried.

'It was a long time ago,' Damien said placatingly. 'Stop bickering, both of you.'

'Why did your father build a grotto here, after such an accident?' I asked Edwin curiously.

'He didn't create *this* grotto. The mosaic work was done by the Selwyns,' Edwin told me.

'Was Rose very attached to the child who was killed?' I asked.

'No,' Damien told me. 'She was rather an unpleasant little girl, by all accounts. The whole thing was hushed up by Rose's father; I heard that he put Miss Jessel into a private nursing home.'

'Of course he did,' Edwin replied smoothly. 'He inherited a vast sum of money that would have gone to Edith had she lived. He didn't want any scandal attached to her death. Poor Vinnie!'

'Let's go,' I said, shivering. 'It's damp and chilly in here.'

I was glad to be out in the comforting warmth of the sun again. As I stepped into the carriage, Bella Careena looked at my neck, and said:

'What has happened to the locket you were wearing when we left the house, Flora?'

Hastily, I put my hand to my throat. The locket had gone. Horrified, I groped for the chain.

'I've lost it!' I whispered, stricken.

Chapter 4

'It must be found at once,' Ruan said. 'You *could* have dropped it in the grotto; I'll go and look.'

'Perhaps it fell on the beach,' Bella said.

'I'll look on the beach,' Edwin said.

'*I* will return to the tower,' Damien said to me, with a reassuring smile. 'Don't worry, Flora. I am sure we shall find your locket.'

I turned my back on the coachman, and fumbled inside my dress; I shook out my skirts and even investigated the inside of the parasol. In vain.

'Are you *very* worried?' Bella asked, watching me as I searched.

'Naturally,' I said shortly. 'Would you not be concerned if you had lost something of great sentimental value?'

'Strange things happen here,' she murmured.

'Such as?'

'Well, like people losing things; odd accidents. Not recently, but long ago.

Now they are happening again. Perhaps you are not meant to be here at all.'

'Why do you dislike me so much?' I challenged her.

'I don't!' she muttered, red-faced.

'Yes you do, Bella Careena. I came here at your mother's invitation, to help her with preparations for Ruan's coming-of-age, and to be a companion to you.'

'I don't *need* a companion!'

'Your mother evidently thought otherwise.'

'I like to be by myself!' she cried angrily.

'I understand that; so do I—often; but you must see that it is not good for *anyone* to be alone all the time.'

'I have mama for company—Edwin, Ruan, Damien; papa, when he is well enough. Nanny Radford. *Lots* of people.'

'I ought to tell your mama that you do not want me to be your companion. You should have told her so yourself when she first suggested it.'

'I *did* tell her! She wouldn't listen to me. When she had your letter, she was *so* excited!'

'Because she enjoys having visitors, I daresay.'

'If you're just a visitor, why did she say you belonged here?' Bella Careena demanded.

'I don't know, Bella Careena. I looked forward to coming here. I have wanted to see this island ever since I saw some sketches of it in my father's book. I have no intention of staying here for good.' We walked to the shade of a tree, and sat there. She leaned back on her elbow, plucking at blades of grass.

'I don't want to go away from this island,' she muttered. 'If I had my way, I would stay forever.'

'I don't think that would be a good idea, Bella; you should see what the world outside is like.'

She turned her back towards me, and stared up at the sky. It seemed a very long time before I saw Ruan and Edwin walking back towards us.

They shook their heads sympathetically.

'There is no trace of the locket in the grotto,' Ruan told me. 'Edwin searched the beach thoroughly, and found nothing. Perhaps Damien will have better luck.'

'It could have got wedged in a rock or something,' Bella pointed out.

'I shall come back to search again, if

Damien is unsuccessful,' Ruan assured me.

It was some time before Damien returned, looking downcast.

'I am sorry, Flora,' he said ruefully. 'I have searched the tower, the steps, the ground at the bottom; and there is no trace of your locket.'

'Don't worry, Flora,' Ruan said reassuringly. 'Mama will instruct the grooms and the servants to search for it; the locket cannot be lost, merely mislaid.'

Bella looked at me gloomily, and said:

'I suppose you don't want to see the Peacock Grotto, now?'

'Of course I do,' I replied, hiding my anxiety behind a smile.

We got into the carriage; the path wound inland, through a miniature forest of tall firs, crowding so close that they shut out the light, giving us a few moments of blessed coolness before we entered a clearing surrounded by sweet-scented, flowering shrubs.

The Grotto of the Peacocks was in the centre of the clearing; a stone temple, with paintings of peacocks on the walls, and a map of the island made in mosaic work on the floor. A stone bench ran around the inside of the walls.

'This was a birthday present from mama to papa,' Bella told me. 'Edwin's father engaged an artist to paint the walls.'

'An artist of great skill,' Edwin conceded, with satisfaction. Everywhere, on the island, was evidence of his father's work; it was surely Edwin who had a right to feel he belonged here, I reflected.

It was only a short walk from the Peacock Grotto to the square-towered church.

The church was old and tranquil, as churches should be; around it the grass was kept neatly trimmed, and on the leaning tombstones I could trace the names of previous owners of the island, as well as servants and estate workers, all their graves neatly kept, and some with wild flowers growing on them.

There was a large tomb in one corner of the little churchyard; it had cherubs' faces carved on one side, and an angel stood on the top, with bowed head. The stone had been mellowed and worn by time, but the inscription on one side was clear enough.

Bella Careena read the words aloud:

Now will I make fast my heart unto yours this day; so that my heart shall be as a ship that is anchored in a quiet harbour, nor shall it venture upon the high seas again; but be forever made fast by this, our troth.

As Bella Careena finished speaking, the silence was complete; the sun burned in the hot blue sky, the five of us seemed locked fast in a spell, charmed to sleep like the courtiers in the old fairy tale.

Ruan broke the spell; he said:

'This is Ann Churnock's tomb; she lived here alone, in the seventeenth century. Some say her true love deserted her, and never kept his promise to marry her; other records state that he was a Royalist killed in the first battle of the Civil War, in August 1642. Whatever the truth of it, after his death, she cut herself off from the world and lived here with only one servant. She made it her business to protect the wild life of the island, and she made lists of all the plants and flowers, and herbs and trees.'

We went into the little church, to which the preacher came every Sunday, when the weather permitted, to take a service. It was cool and dim inside, with heavily-carved pews, two stained glass windows depicting the Creation and the Resurrection, in rich, jewel-like colours; and a splendid marble effigy of a knight in armour lying beside his lady.

'We don't need the carriage now,' Bella Careena said. 'We can walk to my house from here, easily.'

So the carriage was dismissed and we all walked to the cottage in the grounds of the House of the Four Winds.

It was very much a Hansel-and-Gretel sort of cottage, with ornate woodwork and a small balcony; it was secluded, being half hidden by a thick clump of tall firs.

Nanny Radford appeared as we reached the carved door of the little cottage.

She was a small, upright woman, with a faded look about her, as though she had been pressed between the leaves of a book for years, and forgotten. Hair and skin seemed to be the same shade of grey, but her eyes were bright; when Bella Careena introduced us, Nanny Radford put out a hand, and the fingers lay, dry and cool, in mine for a moment.

'We're tired and thirsty, Nanny,' Bella Careena said. 'Please ask Anne to bring us a tray of tea.'

Nanny was not so deaf as poor Dowte;

111

she nodded and went into the house, calling for the servant.

'Come and see *my* house, Flora,' Bella commanded. 'Mama says you are going to come here and live with me.'

'To stay with you,' I corrected firmly. 'I am not going to spend the rest of my life here.'

The furnishings of the house had the same light delicacy as those at Four Winds. There was an airy freshness about it that I found delightful. Bella showed me the room that was to be mine. It had a balcony, and when I stepped on to it, the trees made everything outside so dim and cool that I could have been standing under the sea.

'We'll look at the Grotto of the Four Winds tomorrow,' she said suddenly. 'It's hot and we've wasted a lot of time looking for your locket.'

She looked at me to see if I was going to rebuke her for her rudeness; when I did not reply, she said, more amiably:

'I shall ask mama if I may show you the Sun Grotto. A stream runs into the Grotto, which is really a cave, and there is a pool there in which mama and papa used to bathe. The water is icy cold, though, and papa must not bathe there with her, any more. It is bad for him.'

We went downstairs to have our tea on the lawn outside the cottage. I did not see Nanny Radford again until we were leaving; she nodded approvingly at me, as I lingered behind the others, to hear her words.

'Good thing you're here, Miss Lindsay. That child needs young company. I can see to her creature comforts, same as always, but her mind is beyond me. She's a strange soul; no real malice in her, mind. Never given me a ha'porth of trouble. Too imaginative, though; you'll bring her to earth.'

'I'm only staying for the summer,' I told her.

'Eh?' She chuckled drily. 'We'll see. If Mrs Jardine wants you to stay for ever, you will.'

Damien and I walked back to the house together; Ruan had an errand to attend to at one of the cottages, and Edwin and Bella walked well ahead of us. I watched her, this tall, good-looking girl, and the tall, good-looking man beside her, his springy dark hair flecked with grey.

'A handsome couple!' Damien murmured wickedly in my ear.

'She is still a child,' I protested, shocked. 'Edwin is old enough to be her father!'

'Such alliances have been known to work well; in a few years, Bella Careena will be a woman,' Damien reminded me.

'I suppose so; after all, Rose is twenty years younger than Jerome,' I said.

'She should not have married him!' Damien said. 'She was not meant to be shut away here with an old man. She is lively, beautiful, gracious; she has wit and style. She would be an asset to any London drawing-room.'

'But Rose insists that she is very happy here. I imagine that this is a kind of Paradise for both of them.'

'Nonsense; Jerome keeps her prisoner,' Damien replied coolly.

'Would you like to live here always?' I asked.

'I should like this to be my Kingdom—yes,' he admitted.

'This island would have been yours if your father had not sold it to Jerome's father,' I said impulsively.

'Yes, I am sorry that my father sold the island—but of what use are regrets? Jerome has been kind enough to give me Seawinds as my own domain here.'

'You like staying here?'

'Very much.'

'And—your wife? Does she share your pleasure in the island?'

'No. Irene prefers London. She is a restless creature and likes a social life.'

'Have you no family?' I asked.

'No. Irene lost a child, a daughter. She was ill for some time afterwards. She did not wish to have other children.'

His face looked as though it had been cut from steel.

'Flora,' he said, abruptly. 'Sooner or later you will discover the truth. I prefer to tell you myself: my marriage to Irene is not a happy one.'

'I am sorry,' I whispered inadequately.

'Few marriages are what they seem to be on the surface,' he replied drily.

I looked at him fleetingly as we walked close together, shoulders almost touching. The tawny eyes were bright and hard; his mouth had harshness in every line at that moment; yet I had never found his magnetism so compelling as I did then.

'You must have loved your wife when you married her,' I said, with a sigh.

His smile was bitter.

'According to Irene, I married her for her money. She told me so, on our honeymoon. It is true that I had little money of my own, and she was very rich; an unfortunate situation, but not an impossible one, I thought. Also on our honeymoon, she informed me that she had married me because, at twenty-six, she was already an old maid, and did not wish to die without a wedding-ring on her finger.'

'How could she say such things?' I protested, horrified. 'No marriage could flourish in such a cruel climate!'

'I should not have mentioned such things to you, but your sympathy loosed my tongue,' he told me drily.

We walked the rest of the way in silence. We reached the house and began to walk up the shallow flight of steps to the terrace; I heard Damien draw a sharp breath, and followed the direction of his glance.

A woman, who had been sitting on the terrace, stood up suddenly, shading her face with a parasol.

'Irene!' he murmured, astonished.

She stayed where she was, as still as a statue; I had time to note every detail as we slowly came closer to her.

Irene Ashley was small and slender; she was expensively dressed in cream silk which did nothing for her pale skin, light-coloured eyes and fawn-coloured hair. She was a colourless creature, as colourless as clear water; the more so in contrast to Damien with his powerful build, his air of vitality, his bright gold hair and unusual eyes.

'Irene!' He made no move to embrace her. 'I understood that you intended to remain in London for several days to clear up matters that needed your attention!'

'I *have* attended to them, more quickly than I expected to, my dear Damien.' Her voice was as quiet as her personality. 'There were—certain documents needing my signature.' The smile was edged with faint malice, as though she was enjoying herself. 'I have been at pains to safeguard the little money I have left,' she added.

'*Irene!*' he said curtly. 'You show a deplorable lack of good manners in embarrassing Miss Lindsay thus!'

She turned, giving me a long, assessing glance.

'Ah; so *this* is Miss Lindsay, the new governess.'

'I am not a governess,' I replied calmly. 'I am here to assist Mrs Jardine in preparing for her son's coming-of-age, and to be a companion to Bella Careena.'

Her delicate eyebrows rose.

'A very odd child. I am sure you will find her a handful. So you are not a governess, but an employee of the Jardines, nonetheless.'

'If you wish to put it that way,' I said, disliking her more with every minute that passed.

Colour stung her face, making her look less like a wax doll. I felt the air crackle with the anger that raced between us.

'Miss Flora Lindsay's father was a friend of the Jardines,' Damien told his wife, his voice smooth and cold as marble.

'Really?' She turned an indifferent shoulder towards him and smiled sweetly at me. 'I have to tell you, Miss Lindsay, that Mr Jardine wishes to see you in his study. I am sure you should not keep him waiting.'

As I walked across the terrace, I heard her say, in a high, clear voice:

'I understand that Seawinds is not ready for us, and that we shall be staying here for a day or two...how pleasant!'

I was shaking with anger, as I stepped into the big, book-lined study that was so like my father's; I composed myself with a great effort.

Jerome greeted me warmly; I thought what a fine-looking man he was, with his thick waves of silvery hair, and the piercing dark eyes set in the craggy face.

'Flora, my dear! I hear you have had the misfortune to lose your locket,' he said, full of concern.

'The news has indeed travelled quickly,' I replied, surprised.

'Edwin told me moments ago; and so I asked Irene if she would send you to me as soon as you reached the house.'

I filled in the few details I had concerning the loss of my locket; he listened intently.

'I will have those places searched thoroughly. I am sure it will be found. Edwin said it was of considerable importance to you, because it contained your mother's photograph,' he said.

'The only one that I possess.'

'It *shall* be found,' he insisted. 'Well, my dear—how do you like our beloved island?'

'Very much. It is beautiful; its legends are fascinating.'

119

'Do you think you would be happy living here permanently?' he asked.

His scrutiny was so intense that I moved uneasily.

'It is, perhaps, too soon to say,' I replied cautiously.

'Ah; you are wise to reserve judgment at this stage! Remember, though, that your happiness is important to Rose; and, therefore, to me.'

'Why?' I asked bluntly.

'Because I liked and respected your father, and now you are alone in the world,' he replied.

'I know that you and Rose have been very happy here,' I said.

'Yes.' He nodded. 'We were married in the little church here, when she was eighteen and I was thirty-eight; many predicted that the age gap between us was too great, but we have confounded the doubters! Our summer idyll has lasted for twenty-three years. When Ruan marries and brings his wife here, I hope that they—and their children—will be blessed with such happiness as Rose and I have known.'

I thought that he looked tired and grey as he leaned back in his chair.

'Is there a doctor living on the island?' I asked him.

'No. If anyone is ill, we send the boat to fetch Dr Samuels from Tolfrey. Rarely is the weather so rough, or the fog so thick, that the boat cannot make the journey; in any event, Mrs Clegg is highly skilled in medical matters and I swear she is as good as any doctor. Now, Flora, there remains the question of your salary...'

When I tried to stammer a protest, he waved my words away with a smile.

Upstairs in my room, I wrote a letter to Alexander Arkwright, having been told by the maid who looked after me that the mail was taken across to the mainland every afternoon at four o'clock.

I gave Alexander only the briefest details, telling him I had been most kindly received and was being well looked after; then I took my father's sketchbook from the small writing case of his that I had begun to use since his death, and thumbed through it.

The drawings took on a new life; I recognised one of the trees near the church, bent into a curious shape, like a figure crouching to spring. There was a peacock, the facade of the ruined chapel which I had yet to see, the folly with its ivy-covered walls, and Seawinds.

I left the sketchbook on the dressing table whilst I made preparations for dinner. I wished I had a trunkful of pretty clothes. Instead, I had to make do with a lavender muslin gown trimmed with violet ribbons; I felt as dowdy as any governess or paid companion.

When I went downstairs, Edwin was at the bottom of the staircase, watching my descent.

'I think I shall call you Philomena,' he said lightly. 'It suits you.'

'Do let me put you out of your misery...' I began.

'No,' he retorted. 'I have no wish to be put out of my misery. I wallow in it. I am like these young ladies who happily enjoy the pangs of unrequited love!'

Rose did not put in an appearance at dinner. Jerome seemed perturbed and said if her headache persisted, he would summon Dr Samuels in the morning.

Irene acted as hostess, very graciously, sitting small and upright in her carved chair, and treating me with great condescension.

Edwin and Irene seemed to get on very

well, I noticed. She responded with a show of animation to his enquiries as to her health and the state of London, yet she was aloof and cool when she spoke to her husband.

Jerome mentioned the fifth grotto, asking me if I knew the story of it; when I shook my head, he said:

'Edwin's father decided to build it as a special tribute to Rose. He would not tell me any of the details. She was quite excited; she loved surprises. Sir Marcus had the island to himself for several weeks, whilst Rose and I were in London; he wrote and told us, just before we returned, that it was finished; but when we landed, we discovered, to our distress, that Sir Marcus had been taken ill. He never recovered consciousness.'

I looked at Edwin; his face was impassive. His eyes met mine, and he said:

'As a result of my father's sudden death, the location of the grotto remains a secret. He wrote me, once, concerning it, just before he was taken ill, saying that he considered it his finest piece of work. That is why I am so anxious to discover its whereabouts.'

'Couldn't the workmen have told you?'
I asked.

'The men—there were three of them—
had finished their work and gone, by the
time we returned,' Jerome pointed out.
'They were not local men; I had no way
of tracing them. There was also an artist
specially commissioned by Sir Marcus, but
I did not know his name.'

Bella Careena stared down at her plate,
frowning. The thought occurred to me
that perhaps she alone, amongst all of
them, knew where the grotto was to be
found, and did not intend to reveal her
knowledge.

I was tired out by the events of the day
and glad enough to go to bed. I fell
asleep almost at once, but awoke, some
time later, to find the room full of light.

Rose was standing by the dressing table,
holding my father's sketchbook in her
hand, turning over the leaves very slowly;
she wore a loose wrapper, her beautiful
hair lay like cloth of gold about her
shoulders, and her face was like ivory.
On the dressing table beside her was
the oil lamp she had carried into the
room.

As I sat up in bed, she turned and smiled faintly.

'Are you feeling better?' I asked.

'A little.' I sensed the effort behind the smile. 'I am sorry, Flora, dearest, I did not mean to disturb you—I came to satisfy myself that you had been made comfortable, and I saw the book. I could not resist looking at the sketches. How well I remember your father's love of making drawings, and his skill with a pencil...'

'Your eyes are full of tears,' I said slowly.

She made no reply; instead, she picked up a small box lying beside the lamp, and handed it to me.

'I have brought you a gift, Flora; I intended to leave it by your bedside for you to find when you awoke.'

She handed me the box; it was made of leather; when I opened it, I saw a locket lying on the velvet pad. It was a much more elaborate one than the locket I had lost—it hung from a thick chain, and was heavily chased.

'For you,' she said softly. 'I know that it cannot replace the one you have lost, but I should like you to have it. It belonged to Caspar Jardine's mother.'

'It is beautiful!' I stammered. 'But—I—cannot...it is too valuable...'

'Nonsense. I *want* you to have it, my dear,' she said emphatically.

'I am sure that my own locket will be found.'

'Then you will have two lockets!' She smoothed back the hair from my forehead, as though I was no older than her daughter.

'Wear it, Flora. Enjoy it, as young people should enjoy pretty things,' she said, adding: 'Your father's sketches are very good...'

'When I first saw them, I knew I had to come to the island,' I told her. 'It was a strange compulsion that I cannot explain.'

'Have you been disappointed in our island, Flora?'

'No. I love it.'

'As I do. Everything here is perfect; unchanging!' she whispered, with a vehemence that surprised me. 'You may say that nothing changes, but here time walks more slowly than anywhere else in the world. I felt so safe here!'

'You speak in the past tense,' I said. 'Do you no longer feel safe?'

She hesitated; I thought how pale she looked, how sad she seemed. With an effort, she said:

'So long as I have Jerome, and we have the island and our children, *nothing* can hurt us! I know that! Ruan is young and restless; he will not be content to stay here always, and I don't want Jerome to be burdened with that knowledge until it is absolutely necessary—he has such plans for Ruan, such ideals for the future of the people who live here. Bella, now, is different; she has no wish to leave. I hope you two will be great friends.'

She bent and kissed me.

'Goodnight, Flora, dear,' she whispered.

I did not wear the locket next morning; it was rather too elaborate a piece of jewellery to accompany the simple gown I wore.

I breakfasted alone in the small morning-room; Bella Careena stepped into the room as I was finishing my meal. She wore a simple white dress, on the bodice of which had been sewn several bows of scarlet ribbon; the hem was hung with silver bells that clashed softly as she moved.

'You look very attractive,' I told her.

'I have seen a picture of Ann Churnock,'

she told me unexpectedly. 'She wore a dress like this, with bells on it, so that the birds and animals could hear her coming to feed them.'

'Oh? Where is this picture?'

A secretive smile edged her lips.

'I can't tell you that,' she said. 'Come along, Flora. It's a lovely day, much too nice to stay indoors.'

A familiar figure appeared in the doorway; it was Damien, the sun making a golden halo of his thick curls. My heart leapt at the sight of him.

He wished us good-day, and said to Bella Careena:

'You cannot appropriate Flora for the whole day. I am going to take her rowing on the lake this afternoon.'

'By yourself?' Bella asked disapprovingly.

He looked amused.

'Irene doesn't like the water—you know that. She wants to try her skill at the archery butts, and—on this island, at least—no one is required to provide a chaperone.'

Excitement ran like quicksilver in my veins at the prospect of an afternoon spent exclusively in Damien's company. Bella Careena looked taken aback; Damien smiled at her, and said:

128

'Your papa proposes to give you a French lesson this afternoon, I understand. You must be educated as befits a young lady about to take her place in society.'

'I am not going to take my place in society!' she replied stormily.

'Be that as it may, your papa expects you to present yourself at his study after lunch,' Damien retorted, unperturbed.

She ignored him.

'Let's go to the Sun Grotto, Flora,' she said. 'I have mama's permission. You are favoured, for she rarely allows anyone to go there.'

Damien touched my arm lightly as I passed him.

'I shall look forward to this afternoon,' he told me.

Just beyond the house was a gate set in thick shrubbery; on the other side was a grassy clearing where targets had been set up for archery practice. There was a small building, no more than a shed, where folding chairs were stacked, together with bows and arrows. The shed was locked.

'You need very strong wrists for archery,' Bella told me knowledgeably. 'Papa used to be quite good, though Ruan prefers a rifle, like Damien. Edwin is quite good at archery, but it's my mother and Irene who are best of all; isn't that strange? They often have competitions.'

Beyond the archery butts was the rifle range, again with its small outbuilding. I noticed the padlock on the door, and Bella Careena told me:

'Laurie Perkins has the key; my father is very strict about keeping guns and arrows locked up. We haven't got a gunroom in the house—it's been made into a sitting-room for mama.'

The path along which we walked ended in a small headland, where bushes grew, and gorse hung out its yellow banners, together with the paler gold of wild tree lupins; the path narrowed and became sandy as it wound between the bushes and then sloped down to a deserted sickle of beach.

'This is mama and papa's most private grotto,' Bella Careena announced importantly.

Once again, natural surroundings had been used. There was a wide-mouthed, shallow cave just high enough for a tall man to stand upright inside it; it was empty except for two stone seats; right in the centre was natural rocky pool, fed by a silver stream of water that trickled into it from the back of the cave and overflowed to form a small rivulet that ran down the beach.

'Mama and papa used to come here to bathe early in the mornings,' Bella Careena explained. 'That's why no one else is allowed here. Mama says it's lovely when the sun rises, and shines right into the cave. Come!' She dipped her hands in the water that filled the shallow pool and splashed her face with it.

'You do it,' she said solemnly.

'What on earth for?' I asked, astonished.

'It might make you beautiful. I call this The Pool of Venus,' Bella Careena told me.

I put my hands in water so cold that it made my wrists ache, and then I splashed the icy drops over my face.

On the way back to the house, we looked at the last grotto: it was in a clearing near the house, a marble temple, with a pagoda-like roof, and the sides open to the wind and weather that blew up the Channel. There was a stone seat in the centre of the temple, and four statues stood facing different ways: the North Wind, an old man with a craggy face and a wild mane of hair; the East Wind, a young man with his head lifted as though to the morning; and I was surprised that the South and West Winds had been depicted as women, which was most unusual: the South Wind reminded me of Rose, a summer creature with rounded limbs and a serene face; she looked straight across the sparkling blue waters of the English Channel; whereas the West Wind was a plump, more mature-looking woman, her tranquil gaze fixed on the hazy outline of the Devon coast.

I was entranced.

'This is the work of a very gifted sculptor,' I said.

'Oh, yes; it was for mama's second wedding anniversary, so it had to be just right,' Bella Careena pointed out.

The whole island had been made into a bower for Rose, so dearly had Jerome Jardine loved her, I thought.

'I hope you have enjoyed yourself,' Bella added, with a return to her usual aloofness.

'Very much, thank you.'

'Mama said that I was to look after you.' She sounded piqued.

I sighed.

'Bella, I do want us to be friends. Will

132

you believe me when I say I have no wish to try to get you to leave here?'

'Ruan said your coming was the thin end of the wedge.'

'No. I shall go away from here at the end of the summer.'

'If I grow to like you, I shall not want you to go,' she said candidly.

I laughed, highly amused.

'Thank you, Bella! It's a great comfort to know that!'

I found my locket, just before lunch.

I had gone for a walk to the Peacock Grotto, because I wanted to study its paintings more closely than I had been able to do on the previous day.

It was very quiet; much too quiet, everywhere, except for that occasional ugly screech, heard in the distance. I had the uncanny feeling that I was being followed, yet when I turned my head sharply, there was absolutely no one in sight.

As I stepped into the grotto, I completely forgot my intention of studying the paintings and the map; for my eyes caught a gleam of gold under the stone seat that edged the walls...

I bent and reached for the gold. It was

my locket. I straightened, holding it in my hand, looking at it with tears in my eyes.

The chain was broken; that had probably happened when I lost it. The locket that dangled from the severed chain looked as though it had been flattened by a heavy heel.

Deliberately, I wondered bitterly? Of course. How else? Not only was the delicate gold marked, the tiny pearls crushed, but the photograph of my mother was missing.

Rose and her son were standing in the hall, talking, when I returned to the house; silently, I held out the locket on the palm of my hand.

'Oh, my dear!' Rose picked it up, distressed. 'Where did you find this?'

'In the Peacock Grotto.'

'It seems to have been deliberately damaged,' Ruan said, examining it.

'The photograph has been taken out!' I said bitterly.

'*Who* has done this?' Rose whispered. '*Why?*'

'I don't know,' I said wearily. 'Someone must dislike me very much.'

'That's ridiculous,' Ruan said sharply.

'Leave it with me, Flora; I will see if I can have it repaired next time I go to the mainland.'

'It's beyond repair,' I told him.

'There is a jeweller in Dorchester who does the most skilful repairs,' he told me gently. 'Don't despair until you have seen what he can do. I wish I could restore the picture of your mother; that, alas, I cannot do.'

Nevertheless, I was touched by his kindness.

At lunch, Irene said:

'Dear me! It all seems most odd and inexplicable. Poor Miss Lindsay loses her locket and someone treads on it; furthermore, the picture of her mother has been removed. *Is* all this true, Miss Lindsay?'

'Quite true,' I said distantly, meeting her bright, mocking eyes that reminded me, startlingly, of the eyes of the peacock I had seen that morning.

'A most unpleasant occurrence,' Jerome said shortly. 'I should like to find the culprit.'

'Naturally,' Irene agreed. She smiled across the table and said:

'I understand that my husband is taking you rowing on the lake this afternoon?'

'Yes,' I said.

'I prefer dry land to water. I shall test my skill at the archery butts. I am out of practice, but you would be astonished if you knew the strength in these frail-looking wrists, Miss Lindsay!' she answered.

I looked at her thin wrists; at the long, white fingers, heavy with rings; and, finally, at the face, calm, smiling, watchful...

Damien and I walked from the house to the lake.

'I share Rose's distress at the accident to your locket,' Damien said.

'Bella talks of curses and ghosts,' he added.

'I am sure that both exist only in her imagination.'

'Oh, the island has quite a violent history; I once read that deeds of violence and great tragedies breed ghosts in the minds of those who are finely attuned to such things!'

'I am a very practical young woman!' I assured him.

'Not too practical, I hope,' he teased.

The lake was like a mirror; it was not

very large, and on the far side of it, willows trailed green fingers in the water, as though to cool them. One of the boats had been taken from the boathouse and made ready for us; there was a seat in the stern with a cushion placed in readiness for me. Damien stepped into the boat and helped me down, holding me firmly. His nearness made my breath catch painfully in my throat, and my heart beat wildly.

Damien rowed well, with strong, sure strokes; a couple of wild ducks skimmed the surface of the water and veered away, seawards; overhead two gulls dipped and soared and uttered their strange, harsh cries.

'Ruan does not share Bella Careena's all-absorbing passion for this island,' I said drily.

'Ruan is a young man, with his life before him; it would not be right for him to be incarcerated here,' Damien said briskly.

He rowed across to the far side of the lake.

'We'll leave the boat here and walk in the woods,' he said.

I gave him my hand as I stepped from the boat; his fingers closed very firmly on mine; and then something came hurtling across the lake with a thin, whistling noise. I heard the hiss of air as it almost brushed my cheek. In the nick of time, Damien ducked, still keeping hold of my hand, and the speed of his movement made the boat rock wildly.

The whistling noise stopped suddenly, followed by a piercing, inhuman scream that made my blood run cold; the boat almost capsized as I tried desperately to scramble ashore. Damien lifted me bodily from my feet, and for a split second, I lay against his broad, powerful chest, shaken and terrified. I heard a horrible, strangled sound from the trees behind us.

'What was it?' I whispered.

'An arrow,' Damien replied grimly; he helped me up the bank, until we stood on firmer ground. He glanced over his shoulder, briefly.

'Don't look, Flora,' he commanded.

It was too late; I had already seen the dead peacock lying beneath a tree, an arrow embedded in its bright, beautiful plumage.

I felt giddy and nauseated; Damien held me close as I bent my head, shivering, remembering that he had told me the place was a bird sanctuary.

'We'll go to Seawinds,' he told me. 'However, first we'll pay a visit to Laurie Perkins' forge. It's only just across the lake, near the boathouse. He is responsible for the safe custody of the guns and arrows.'

His jaw was hard; he kept hold of my arm very firmly, as we skirted the path that led around the lake; within a short time, we had reached a rather secretive-looking cottage, and beside it, a small forge.

Damien rapped at the door of the cottage; there was no reply. We went into the forge; the fire was low, the bellows idle. A couple of horseshoes had been nailed to the walls. The smith's implements lay beside the nearly-dead fire, together with some pieces of fancy wrought iron. On a bench, I saw four arrows. Beside them was a bow, which would be used to test the sharpness of the arrows once they had been sharpened.

'Surely Laurie Perkins must know that Jerome would be extremely angry with him for killing a peacock?' I said.

'Perhaps the arrow was aimed at me,' Damien replied shortly.

'Who would do such a thing?' I demanded, in shocked disbelief.

'I don't know.' He shrugged. 'Perhaps it was meant to frighten me.'

'You could have been killed!' I whispered.

'Would it have mattered very much to you, Flora?' Damien asked softly.

Before I could reply, we heard the sound of footsteps on the path outside; a shadow darkened the doorway.

He was a man of about thirty, short, well-muscled and stocky; he had a shock of wild black hair, a broad, tanned face, and wore working clothes.

'Lookin' for me?' he asked.

Chapter 5

Damien looked shrewdly at the figure in the doorway.

'How many arrows did you bring here to sharpen, Perkins?' he asked.

'Five—sir.'

I didn't like Laurie Perkins' manner; there was no deference in it.

'There are four arrows here,' Damien pointed out.

'Then it seems one's bin taken, don't it?' Perkins replied smoothly.

'Someone shot an arrow at me, as I was stepping from the boat,' Damien told him. 'It missed me; it has killed a peacock.'

'There's bad luck, then,' Perkins replied impassively. 'At least, so 'tis said. Kill one of them birds, and no good will follow on it. Who done it, sir?'

The bold black eyes stared unwinkingly at Damien.

'Dammit, man, I might have been injured! So might Miss Lindsay!' Damien cried angrily.

141

'Or killed, sir. Them arrows has all bin sharpened. I'm about to test 'em,' Perkins answered.

'Whoever loosed the arrow could only have done so from a bow,' Damien pointed out.

'Well, sir, there's the bow, as you see.' Perkins pointed to the bench. 'Someone must 'ave bin nippy to try a spot o' target practice and then put the bow back, for I ain't been gone more 'n 'arf an 'our.'

'Where were you?' Damien demanded.

'At *your* 'ouse, Mr Ashley, *sir!*' The voice was frankly surly. 'Mrs Jardine sent for me. There's something wants doin' to one o' the latches on the garden door. She's there, now, sir, why don't you check for yourself, and you'll see I'm speakin' the truth? I've better things to do, Mr Ashley, than try me skill with them arrows except on the proper target; and better respect for Mr Jardine than to go killin' 'is peacocks!'

He stood aside pointedly for us to leave; I saw the tightness of Damien's mouth, and I could still feel Perkins' eyes on my back as we walked out of the forge.

'Do you think he was lying?' I whispered, as soon as we were out of earshot.

'Hardly likely. How could he have

142

sprinted back and returned the bow?'

'Who would have a grudge against you?' I asked, still unhappy.

'I don't think it was meant for either of us,' he answered. 'Not in the sense of being a lethal weapon, anyway; someone was trying to annoy or frighten us.'

We passed into the dimness of a tiny forest of trees, Damien walking so close to me that his shoulder touched mine, but I could not recapture the pleasure I had previously felt in the afternoon and the company.

The trees thinned; we came upon Seawinds, doors and windows open to sun and fresh air. We went straight to the sitting room and found Rose, giving instructions to a servant.

She looked surprised to see us: when she had dismissed the servant, Damien told her what had happened. I saw disbelief and horror on her face.

'You cannot seriously think it was Perkins!' she said. 'He *is* telling the truth. I came over here to see that all was in order for you and Irene to move in; and I gave him instructions about the latch.'

'Where is Mrs Ashley?' I asked.

'I left her at the butts, with Edwin.'

Rose looked at me, troubled. 'Ruan has gone fishing with one of the Clegg boys, Jerome is working in his study on the farm accounts. There is only one person I cannot account for; Bella Careena has been missing all the afternoon. She didn't go to Jerome for her French lesson and when he sent one of the servants to look for her, she was nowhere in the house or cottage. Nanny declares there has been no sign of her since before lunch.

'I'll look for her,' I offered.

'How will you know where to look?' she asked doubtfully.

'I don't know; I'll try the Shell Grotto first.'

'Will you have some tea before you leave, Flora?'

I shook my head. Damien said he would take tea with her; as I was leaving the house, Rose said unhappily:

'I think perhaps we could keep the incident of the peacock from Jerome. It will only anger and distress him to know what has happened.'

'Of course,' Damien agreed, at once. 'It was probably an unpleasant practical joke that could have had dire consequences. Let's forget the whole business.'

I took the path to the grotto. Ahead of me was the gap in the bushes that led to the beach path; away to my left I glimpsed the ruined chapel that I had not yet explored, and I wondered suddenly if Bella Careena had gone there.

A narrow earth track led under the trees to the chapel; it was not far away, but when I came upon it, I shivered, disliking the place. It was very silent; there was no birdsong, no sign of life; only crumbling walls, netted in ivy, with gaps where there had been windows and doors, and no roof.

I returned to the cliff-path, and stood at the gap in the bushes looking below me. I was nimble-footed enough to climb down to the beach without fear of mishap, but my dislike of heights affected me strongly and I wished there was someone with me.

'Bella Careena!' I called. Only the soft shush-shush of the waves on the sands answered me; but I thought I heard another sound—the faint tinkling of bells.

I took a long, steadying breath, and tried not to think of poor little Edith, whose untimely death had made Wilfrid Brandon rich, and sent a distracted governess almost

145

out of her mind. Carefully, I made my way down the path until I came to the rocky ledge.

She was there; sitting at the cave entrance, arms crossed around her knees. She smiled happily at me, and patted the sun-warmed stone beside her.

'Come and look at the sea, Flora,' she said. 'I am waiting for the sun to come round and light up the mermaid's eyes, and make the sea-serpent look like a real one.'

I was angry with her.

'You heard me call, yet you did not answer,' I accused. 'People have been looking for you! Here you are, comfortably tucked away enjoying yourself, when you are supposed to be having a French lesson with your father!'

She sighed.

'Oh, Flora, don't be governess-y! I know papa will be cross, he'll lecture me, and I shall have to do extra French for a penance.'

'So this isn't the first time you've played truant?'

'Of course it isn't! Everyone plays truant sometimes. DO sit down, just for a minute, please, Flora.'

I sat down, reluctantly; the roof of the cave overhung the ledge sufficiently to give a welcome shade.

'Why aren't you with Damien?' Bella Careena asked.

I hesitated; she saw my hesitation and pounced.

'Something happened; what?'

'Damien and I were rowing on the lake when someone shot an arrow across and killed a peacock, close to us.'

Her eyes were like saucers.

'It's terribly unlucky to kill a peacock! It brings down a curse on the island.'

'Don't be silly!' I cried, exasperated; the afternoon that had begun so happily had ended in disaster, and—following upon the discovery of my broken locket—it was all too much for me. I felt wretched.

'Perhaps the peacock was killed by the person who broke your locket,' Bella said reflectively.

Her eyes were on the horizon; below us the blue waters of the bay preened themselves in the sunshine, and tiny white waves spread their lace along the beach; but I had little heart for the beauty all around me.

'There is a serpent in every Garden of

Eden,' Bella said matter-of-factly.

'Who told you that?' I asked.

'Edwin; last time he was here. I told him that mama and papa call this place their Garden of Eden and that's when he made the remark about the serpent.' She gave me a very childlike scrutiny, adding:

'Ruan likes you, doesn't he?'

'So you say. I've been here scarcely two days and he hardly knows me,' I pointed out.

'Ruan will have to find a wife soon. I heard papa tell mama it was time Ruan thought seriously about getting married; mama laughed and said the choice was a bit limited, here on the island; then, soon afterwards, mama invited you here,' she answered.

I stood up, brushing my skirt with a hand that shook a little.

'Come along, there's a good girl. It isn't fair to worry your mama, and she has no idea where you are.'

Reluctantly, Bella rose to her feet; the beach suddenly seemed very far below me, and I put my hand to my forehead as the horizon dipped and swayed in front of me.

Bella caught my arm in a firm grip.

148

'I forgot. You don't like heights, do you? You *do* look pale, Flora; it's all right, you're quite safe. You won't tumble over like poor, silly, Edith Freemantle did. Perhaps it was punishment on her—she was so horrid to poor Vinnie, the governess. I'd hate to be a governess or a companion; it's just a sort of servant, really. Mama said she never wanted to see *anyone* treated as poor Vinnie was. I wish it hadn't happened here, because now mama doesn't like this part of the island a bit. That's because *she* was the one who found poor Edith...'

I wasn't thinking about Edith and her unfortunate governess; I was reflecting, for the first time, that I had never actually seen my birth certificate even though I knew when and where I had been born.

Probably Alexander Arkwright had it, safely locked in his office with my father's will, and a number of other personal documents.

I decided to write and ask him—if it was in his possession—to send it to me.

When Bella and I reached Seawinds, Damien had already left there to return to the House of the Four Winds.

Rose was in the sitting-room; she looked

at her daughter with a mixture of relief and annoyance.

'Go straight home to papa, Bella, and tell him you are sorry you played truant. You know he isn't well; it was wrong of you to worry him so.'

She looked mutinous.

'Can't I wait here until *you* go back?' she muttered.

'No!' said Rose sharply, 'You have really been very naughty, Bella. You can walk home, as a punishment. When you reach the house ask one of the servants to send Dowte with a carriage. Off you go, now!'

Her voice brooked no argument; Bella Careena shrugged philosophically, and left the room. Rose pushed the heavy masses of wheat-gold hair away from her forehead, and looked at me sombrely.

'Flora, there is something I have not told anyone. A secret I have kept to myself for weeks. I *cannot* tell my family. It would be a relief to tell *you!*'

'Your confidence is safe with me,' I promised.

Her eyes were full of tears.

'Jerome has a serious heart condition; the specialist whom he consulted in London told me that my husband could expect to live a couple more years, at the most.'

'Are you certain of this?' I stammered, appalled.

'Absolutely. The consultant left me in no doubt; the decision, he said, was mine: whether or not to tell Jerome and our children the truth. I made my decision. I don't regret it; even though I know that the strain of too much excitement, any serious over-exertion, or a sudden shock, would undoubtedly prove fatal to my husband.'

'Do you think that Jerome suspects?' I asked uneasily.

'No. He has been told to rest and take life more quietly, and not overtax himself, or his heart will protest vigorously. It has not been easy for him to accept physical restrictions, you know. He has always been an active man.'

'Should you not tell Ruan?' I asked.

'I have considered it; and decided not to do so. It will make him unhappy, and that fact will soon be apparent. Jerome would soon ferret the truth from him.'

'What about the coming-of-age celebrations? They will put a strain on Jerome,' I pointed out.

'I shall see that he doesn't overtax himself. I will learn to be even more vigilant than I am now,' she replied, almost ferociously. 'Jerome would be bitterly disappointed, as well as suspicious, if Ruan was not given a splendid welcome to his new status. As for Bella—it would be cruel and pointless to tell *her* the truth; no, Flora—let them all have two years unclouded by sorrow for what will come after!'

'You will find it a heavy burden,' I told her.

'My shoulders are strong. It is a comfort to talk to you.'

'Will you tell Damien and Irene?' I asked.

'No!' she said sharply. 'I do not want them to know!'

'What about Edwin?' I asked.

There was a moment's gentleness in her face.

'Edwin? Yes, a dear friend, Flora, one who could be as understanding as you have been; but I needed to confide in a woman, for who else will understand the nature of my problems half so well? It would distress him very much; he has known Jerome and myself for many years. Let him remain in

152

happy ignorance until the time comes. You see, Flora, I have been selfish in burdening only you!'

'Perhaps I'm better equipped than anyone else,' I told her. 'My mother and my father have both died within the last few years, as you know.'

She nodded, her eyes suddenly full of blue fire.

'Jerome is the one man I have ever truly loved. A man of tenderness and strength, humility and passion. I was a child when I married him, and he was already middle-aged; but he has taught me all I know of every aspect of love between a man and a woman.'

'Love will give you strength to live through the next two years,' I told her.

'One day, *you* will love as I do, Flora. We are alike. There is great capacity for passion tucked away behind the quiet facade of yours!'

'My mother distrusted passion,' I said.

A curious expression crossed her face.

'Was she—a *cold* woman, Flora?' she asked hesitantly.

I shook my head.

'By no means; warm, affectionate, kind; but passion was of the flesh only, she said devotion to one another was the only true love.'

'There *must* be passion, in the love between a man and a woman, Flora. One day, you will understand that.'

I thought it best to change the subject. 'Will Ruan stay here for the next two years?' I asked. She nodded.

'He will stay, Flora. Because I need him here, because Jerome needs him. After Jerome's death, he may do as he pleases, go where he will. It will not matter to Jerome—or to me—then.'

I did not wait for the carriage to collect me from Seawinds. I walked alone, back to the House of the Four Winds. I had a great deal to think about; Rose's news had shocked me greatly, and saddened me. Yet Jerome Jardine would have been the first person to admit that his life had been full and happy.

Before I dressed for dinner, I sat down at my desk and wrote to Alexander Arkwright.

The matter of the arrow was kept from Jerome; at dinner that evening he asked me if I had enjoyed my afternoon, which seemed to greatly amuse Irene. It was a cold kind of amusement; I distrusted her.

After dinner, Jerome went to his room, accompanied by Rose; Damien challenged Ruan to a game of chess and Bella Careena had to return to the cottage to read an hour's French.

The night was so warm that I decided to walk in the grounds. The moon was coming up, silvering the sea with a touch of phantom light. I walked round to the back of the house; the conservatory was in darkness, and I peered through the window. It was like a green jungle inside, the plants pushing against the glass as though trying to escape into the outdoors. The curtains in the study were undrawn, and I could see Ruan and Damien engrossed in their game of chess, looking very companionable.

Two hands came out of the darkness from behind, and fastened themselves firmly on my shoulders. I screamed aloud.

A familiar voice said in my ear:

'Ah! It wasn't fair to startle you, but you should not be alone on such a night!'

I whirled on him so fiercely that his hands were wrenched from my shoulders; I was furiously angry.

'Do you usually spring upon people in the dark?' I choked.

'Oh, come,' Edwin Trehearne said mildly, 'I didn't spring upon you. But perhaps I should have given warning of my approach. It is a fine night; I was going to ask you to walk with me.'

'No thank you!' I retorted.

'Alas! I am not Damien!' he said, with mock dismay.

'That is a mischievous and impertinent remark!' I cried angrily.

'I make no apologies!' His smile was wicked, his teeth gleamed whitely. 'I am merely trying to warn you not to let your heart run away too far and fast.'

'I need no warnings; I am quite capable of managing my own life!'

'There are times when I doubt that, Flora Belle!'

'This is a ridiculous conversation, Edwin Trehearne!'

'I find you interesting,' he replied softly. 'I like your independence, your lively mind. Bella Careena tells me she hopes you will marry Ruan; that will *never* do. He is a boy!'

'*You* are too old for me!' I retorted.

I could have bitten out my foolish,

156

impetuous tongue. It was a cruel remark and I had not meant it. His reaction surprised me.

'Ah yes, Flora! I am seventeen years older than you are; but think of the pleasure that Rose and Jerome have found in one another, despite the difference in their ages! Damien is forty-one, I believe; yet you look upon him with favour. What does he possess that I lack?'

The mockery was savage; without warning, he pulled me close and kissed me, a hard, fierce kiss on my lips. I was outraged; to kiss me like that, as though we were lovers, or at the very least, engaged to be married! It was unforgivable.

I was shivering when he released me, and he laughed.

'No gentleman would behave as you do!' I told him angrily.

'What *is* a gentleman, Flora? A man who conducts himself circumspectly on all occasions? Is that all there is to it?'

He disappeared into the darkness, leaving me thoroughly confused, my lips throbbing, my body still trembling.

In the morning, I told Rose that I was ready to move in to the cottage with Bella;

she seemed delighted.

'Oh, Flora, I am glad you have made the decision—that is an excellent idea. You will be good for her; I like to feel she has someone sensible near her, now that Nanny is growing old.'

If Bella was pleased concerning my decision, she did not say so. One of the servants carried my luggage to the cottage, and Nanny Radford expressed her approval of the move.

Bella sat on the edge of the bed, watching me unpack my possessions.

'I hope you are not going to keep an eye on me all the time,' she said flatly.

'I've no intention of doing so,' I replied briskly. 'I'm going to be busy helping your mama.'

'I like being by myself.'

'You can have plenty of solitude. You won't come to any harm here, on this island.'

'Oh, you're wrong, Flora! All kinds of strange things happen here. People have disappeared. Besides—look what happened to your locket; *someone* did it. Someone shot at you with the arrow. Sometimes I feel eyes watching me, you know.'

'You need to keep a tight hand on that

imagination of yours,' I told her. 'Your mama is expecting you at the house this morning; the dressmaker has arrived from Tolfrey with some materials to be made up for you.'

Bella looked bored, but she slid from the bed, and went across to the house.

That afternoon, I watched Rose and Irene practise their skill with bow and arrow. A small crowd of us gathered; the servants were permitted to watch and they all thoroughly enjoyed the occasion.

Watching them, I realised the strength needed in those fragile-looking wrists, and saw the steadiness of aim, the sharpness of eye that both possessed. The arrow was fitted to the bow; drawn back with care and a deadly steadfastness of purpose. No one moved or spoke; we all seemed to be holding our breath. Not even the peacocks screeched, as the arrow was loosed to go winging cleanly through the air and find targets set up at the end of the butts.

Rose had won. The silence was broken by a small cheer. She smiled at Jerome, who was sitting in a camp chair beside Damien.

The two men took over; Edwin won.

Damien shrugged ruefully and congratulated him. Irene came across to me.

'I hope you have enjoyed watching the game,' she said graciously.

'Very much. Who taught you?'

'A tutor who was once here, a friend of Jerome's. I play when I am in London; I enjoy the sport.'

She sat down beside me. I smelled light flowery perfume. I looked again at the bony wrists and long, delicate-looking fingers. As though she knew what I was thinking, Irene leaned towards me, and encircled my wrist with her fingers.

The strength of the grip made me wince. It caused me intense pain though I would not cry out.

When she released her grip, I said:

'I wonder who shot the arrow that killed the peacock? Or have you not heard about it?'

'I have heard, Miss Lindsay. Rose has a little conspiracy afoot to keep it from Jerome who might be upset about it. How absurd! It was not a good shot; after all, I don't think it was the peacock who was the target, do you?'

'You are not seriously suggesting that the intention was to kill one of us?' I retorted.

'It seems like it, you must admit, Miss Lindsay.'

Her voice was careless, as though the subject had ceased to interest her. She lifted her hand to pat her hair and the diamonds in her ring glittered as coldly as the glass eyes on the wall of the Shell Grotto.

'I should like to kill my husband,' she said coolly.

I stared at her, aghast.

'You should not say such things—especially to someone you regard as an employee, Mrs Ashley,' I told her.

'Touché!' Irene was delighted; she threw back her head and laughed, showing small white teeth. 'Damien knows how much I hate him and finds it amusing. He drags me here, to be with him, when he knows that I am bored with this place and with the people in it who believe they are living in a fairytale that has a happy ending. How stupid, how dull they are!'

Chapter 6

Rose told me that Irene and Damien would be giving a party at Seawinds, and afterwards, there would be a return party at Four Winds.

She looked critically at my only evening dress, of pale lilac, and said:

'There is not time for Miss Hyams to make you something in time for Irene's party, alas; however, there are gowns in my wardrobe that I have not yet worn. I will have one of them altered to fit you.'

I stammered embarrassed protests which she waved away, smiling.

'Accept the loan of a gown as a token of gratitude from me, Flora. Your presence here gives me pleasure, as well as comfort.'

Bella suggested a picnic tea in the Peacock Grotto.

'It's cool there,' she said. 'You know the peacock that was killed? Laurie Perkins said we could use the feathers to decorate the walls. That's a good idea.'

I shivered. It sounded macabre.

The weather was still very hot; Nanny Radford supervised the packing of a picnic basket, but after half an hour in the grotto, Bella grew bored; she wanted to show me things I had missed on my tour of the island: a little tombstone, half-buried in ivy, dedicated to the memory of 'Redwings' a favourite horse.

'That was my first horse,' she said. 'Do you ride, Flora?'

'No. I've never learned.'

'Then you must,' she said, leading me on to a little natural hollow by the banks of a stream; just above the water, almost hidden by ferns, was a little, weatherbeaten stone statue of a Cupid, a chip in one wing, his sightless eyes turned towards us; beyond it, at the end of a small grove, was a round, rustic summerhouse with a thatched roof. The door creaked eerily on its hinges when Bella lifted the latch. Inside, it was empty, smelling of dust and dead leaves.

'You can follow the stream all the way back, you know,' she said.

'Back to where?'

'The grotto.' She sat down, pulling off shoes and stockings.

'I'm going to paddle back along the stream, Flora. It's quite safe, it only just comes over my ankles. Coming? Or are you going to walk back along the path?'

'I'll follow the path,' I said. I couldn't be bothered to strip off my stockings and, anyway, I wanted to be alone with my thoughts.

'See you at the grotto!' she cried.

I stood there watching her until she was out of sight. Silence washed peacefully around me, broken only by the sound of running water.

Once again, I had the feeling that I was being watched; I turned, and looked over my shoulder. A figure stepped on to the path, and my heart leapt.

I saw a tall, muscular man with a thick cap of tawny curls; a sensual lift to his mouth; classic good looks of a profile on a Greek coin; an air of vitality about him, of great power, of strength like a tiger's.

'Flora!' he called, holding out his hands.

I went to him, my heart clamouring furiously; I felt helpless, as though I was drowning, and did not want to save myself.

He put his arm around my shoulders.

'Come!' he whispered.

He led me to the little summerhouse,

smiling as the latch protested at being lifted again. Inside, he gently put his hands on my shoulders and drew me to him. All about us was the warm dusty silence, as he bent his head and kissed me.

It was not a hard kiss such as Edwin had given. It was a slow, warm, exploring kiss that gradually increased in intensity. His lips fastened more firmly on my willing mouth; I was held so close, I could feel his heartbeats.

Never be led away by passion, my mother had said. Words, words! Words to be tossed like leaves on the wind; words that rose and whirled around me like a flock of birds. Passion was a slow fire running in the veins, glowing with terrible intensity, as heartbeats became faster and more uneven, limbs more willing.

Suddenly, he let me go. I felt a bitter disappointment, even whilst I recognised his wisdom in releasing me.

'I make no apology,' he said arrogantly. 'You are truly wonderful, Flora. A woman, not a girl. A woman of warmth, loving and giving. When I first saw you on the quay, I thought you looked like a seabird, wild and free and proud. I have the bird in my hand, but I have to open my hand and let it go

166

for a little while. Do you understand?'

'Yes,' I said, with a sigh. *For a little while?* I wondered at those words.

His voice was harsh when he spoke again:

'I am leaving Irene. I have told you, my marriage is at an end.'

'You will still be tied to her.'

'No.' He drew a deep breath. 'We will not talk of things on such a day as this.'

'I must go,' I said flatly. 'Bella Careena will wonder what has become of me.'

'Tell her that you were lost. After all, is that not true?' His smile was wry.

Briefly, he laid a cool, dry hand against my hot cheek. I saw the longing in his eyes; I wanted him; I knew that he wanted me. We had no future, for divorce was unthinkable. At summer's ending, I must leave Bella Careena and never return.

Perhaps Damien read my thoughts; he bent his head, and told me:

'The summer is young, yet.'

He kissed me again, gently, without passion. Then he lifted the latch and we went outside.

I was up early next morning. For the first time, I wore the locket Rose had

167

given me. It was heavy on its gold rope, the locket hanging almost to my waist. Like mine, there was a hinge on it, but when I opened the locket, there was no photograph inside.

Ruan didn't notice the locket until we were in the boat together; I was watching the island smudged into a blue-green haze on the horizon, wondering if its spell would seem less potent, once I was free of it; and I heard his sharply drawn breath and turned my head towards him. He was looking nonplussed.

'Who gave that to you, Flora?' he asked.

'Your mama; why do you look at me so?'

'It is odd that she should have given you that particular piece of jewellery.'

'She did so when I lost my own locket,' I told him.

'I have your locket with me; I shall instruct Mr Gilford, at the Fortune, to take it into Dorchester for me, in order that it can be repaired. Flora, the piece of jewellery that you are wearing is a family heirloom.'

Embarrassed, I said stiffly:

'Then I will return it to your mother when my own is repaired.'

'No, no, you don't understand.' He came and sat beside me, his face gentle and oddly amused. 'You mustn't think of handing it back; she would be very hurt.'

'Is there something else special about it besides the fact that it is an heirloom?' I asked.

'Yes.' He spoke reluctantly.

'Well?' My voice was tart. 'Is it cursed? Is *that* it? Curses seem to grow along with trees on your island.'

'No, it's not cursed. Don't be cross,' he coaxed. 'It's just that this locket belonged to my great-great grandmother, and, by tradition, it is handed down to the bride of the heir to Bella Careena.'

I was silent, my embarrassment growing; I had to look up, at last, and I met his eyes reluctantly. He was still smiling.

'Perhaps mama was being a little premature,' he said wickedly. 'I *do* rather like you, Flora. I thought perhaps you'd say you liked me, too. Don't look so unhappy. I'm teasing. Flirting with you; hasn't anyone ever done that before?'

'No,' I admitted.

'You're not like most of the women I have met,' he told me. 'They all have their sights firmly set on Holy Matrimony.'

'What other career is there for a woman, unless she has private means?' I argued.

'None, I suppose.' He pursed his mouth thoughtfully. '*You* have to work for your living, Flora; whatever you are, governess, companion, it cannot be an easy life.'

This was dangerous ground; I changed the subject.

'Your mother and father are very happy,' I murmured. 'Their devotion to one another makes a clear statement that a good marriage is a great gift.'

'Yes,' he agreed. 'Mama is content to stay on the island because papa loves it there. Bella Careena is much too involved with the island; at her age, she should be eager to sample the world outside.'

'You told her I had come to take her away from the island!' I accused.

His grin was boyish.

'Oh, I teased her about that, and she took it seriously! Papa is not well, nor is he a young man. I shall stay on the island because of that; but not willingly, Flora; and when I marry, I shall not expect my wife to be content with such a narrow life.'

I sensed his restlessness, his impatience. I looked back at the island. It would never put a spell on Ruan Jardine, I reflected.

'I want to travel all over the world,' he said, with a sigh.

'Then you should not think of marriage,' I retorted. 'Women do not take kindly to wandering around the world with all their possessions in a dress basket. They like to put down roots.'

'Edwin once said the wise men never marry at all,' Ruan told me.

'How cynical; is that why *he* never married?'

'He once told me he was too busy to look for a wife,' Ruan replied. 'He has great estates to look after, in Gloucestershire and Somerset.'

'With no son to inherit them!' I retorted.

'Well—Edwin is a romantic, you know. He told my father that he had never met a woman he wanted to marry. He would not marry simply to produce heirs.'

There was a bustle of activity at the quay when we arrived. Fishing boats were putting out to sea, children were playing on the sands. At the Fortune, casks and barrels of beer were being unloaded; mats were spread over the garden walls of little cottages that straggled up the main street.

It was a pleasant day; Ruan knew

everyone, and at each cottage we visited we were received with great deference. As Rose had assured me, there were plenty of willing volunteers for the task of helping with the coming celebrations. My list was full by lunchtime.

We ate lunch in the cool dining-room of the Fortune; fresh salmon, tiny new potatoes, strawberries picked that morning, thick yellow cream. It was a very pleasant and leisurely lunch.

'I *have* enjoyed today,' I told him.

'Good!' His smile was boyish, with a hint of the maturity yet to come. He leaned forward and looked closely at the oval of gold swinging from its chain against my dress.

'It does suit you, Flora,' he murmured.

I was tired when I returned to the island that evening; the day had been exhausting, as well as delightful. There was no sign of Bella when I reached the cottage.

'Miss Bella has gone for a walk on her own,' Nanny told me. 'Mrs Jardine came and left presents upstairs for you.'

Upstairs, on my bed, were more gifts from Rose; a very pretty dress of ivory silk, tucked and flounced and cut low on the shoulders. There were touches of colour in the skirt, where it was caught up by tiny posies of velvet pansies, amethyst, purple, yellow. A knot of amethyst velvet ribbons trailed long streamers from the bodice. There was a pair of shoes to match the gown and a narrow leather box lying on the bed.

I opened the box, with trembling fingers; inside was a necklace of small, perfectly-matched pearls. The richness of their sheen, their milky depths, proclaimed that they were real.

There was also a note from Rose.

'Dear Flora, please accept these gifts, with my blessing. Wear the dress and the pearls this evening.'

I was deeply troubled; the more so, because Rose believed me to be penniless and, out of a loving generous heart, wanted to share some of her beauty with me.

The little maid came to help me dress; when I was ready, I looked in the mirror, and saw her face reflected there as well as mine. She looked impressed, and admiring.

'Oh, miss, you *do* look lovely!' she said.

Damien was standing in the hall when I reached Four Winds. His tawny eyes were suddenly full of a fire like the sun...

'Flora!' he said softly. 'You look very beautiful.'

'You flatter me,' I murmured.

'Indeed I do not. I wish that *I* could have taken you to the mainland today, instead of Ruan.'

'It would not have been right!' I whispered.

'What is right and what is wrong when two people desire one another?' he demanded. 'If life comes with hands outstretched, offering gifts of joy, are we to dash them from her hands and turn our backs? Opportunities are precious, life is fleeting; yesterday we were young, tomorrow we shall be old. Remember that, Flora. One day you and I will bathe from the Sun Grotto in the early morning.'

'It is not possible,' I replied, trembling.

'All things are possible, if one wishes them to be. Ah, Flora—you are like most women! You fear what you most desire!'

His eyes danced, his voice was mocking, his smile teased me, drew my heart even closer to his...

Our conversation was interrupted by the sudden entrance of Bella, dressed for dinner; she came up to me, and said:

174

'Mama has made you a present of the gold locket that is given to the bride on the day she marries the heir to the island!'

'How do you know that?' I asked as calmly as I could.

'I went to your room to look for you, and it was lying there on the dressing table.' Her eyes were accusing. 'Are you going to marry Ruan? Is that why you came here?'

I drew a deep breath and said:

'I shall marry whom I choose—*when* I am ready to be married!'

There was a grim expression on Damien's face; he said nothing more, as the three of us went across the hall to the drawing-room.

I tried to put the incident out of my mind. I thanked Rose for her gifts of the gown and shoes and pearls, and she told me, happily, that she found pleasure in giving.

As the day of the party approached, there was a great bustle of activity on the island; in the late afternoon, the guests began to arrive, and extra boats had been hired to bring them over.

The guest-list was a long one. A band

had been hired. Several coaches took the people from Four Winds over to Seawinds. It was exciting to drive under the trees, with the stars sparkling in the sky above, the sound of laughter, the rhythm of the horses' hooves all around me; the night air cool against my cheeks, when we came suddenly upon Seawinds, ablaze with lights, the sound of music coming through the open windows.

Irene stood beside Damien, in the hall, receiving the guests. He looked aloof and formal; Irene was more nondescript than ever in a gown of pale-green silk; she seemed weighted down by the jewels at her throat, on her hands, encircling her wrists. Her smile for me was as cold as a winter morning, her greeting perfunctory.

I danced with Edwin; he was an expert dancer, to my surprise. I was clumsy, never having learned to dance.

'You must learn to relax,' he told me. 'Let me guide you. You don't like to be guided, do you, Flora Lindsay?'

I looked sharply at him. There was no way of guessing his thoughts. His dark eyes sparkled, his hold was firm.

'Forget him, Flora!' he whispered. 'No happiness can come from such a liaison as you and he contemplate. There will be no lasting joy in the thoughts and feelings *you* entertain for him!'

'You do not know what I think or feel!' I retorted angrily.

'I know better than you imagine. It is all such a waste. You are infatuated!'

'As always, you talk impertinent nonsense!' I choked furiously.

We did not speak again, and I was glad when the dance ended.

Jerome sat in a splendid carved chair with a scarlet leather seat, watching his wife with open admiration. She was beautiful in yellow silk, with touches of emerald velvet, and rarely left him alone for long, but came over to speak to him after every dance.

I danced next with Damien, aware that Irene's eyes followed us.

'I have missed you, Flora,' he said. 'You have deliberately hidden yourself away from me.'

'No. I have been busy. There is a great deal for me to do.'

'I shall keep my promise; one day, we will bathe from the Sun Grotto,' he told me.

'You know it is a private place.'

'The Jardines do not go there, now. No

one will see us; we can go early, before the sun rises. It will be our secret.'

I was kept busy helping Rose with preparations for a return party at the House of the Four Winds. There was to be a treasure hunt; she would not tell me anything about it; it was something that she and Jerome always planned together, for the amusement of their guests.

On the night of the party, Four Winds was full of flowers. A buffet had been set out in the big supper-room adjoining the ballroom, the band had been re-engaged, the rooms made ready for the overnight guests. Bella Careena was full of the second party, having had a taste of gaiety at Seawinds.

We paired off for the treasure hunt, which was the high spot of the evening. Edwin Trehearne was my partner.

'Ah, poor Flora!' he mocked gently. 'It is not at all to your liking, is it?'

It was a calm, beautiful night, the sky bright with stars, a welcome little breeze blowing in from the sea. From the grounds around the House of the Four Winds came the laughter and triumphant shouts of the

178

searchers as they unearthed clues, and went on to the next one. The servants had placed lighted oil lamps at intervals around the grounds, and the effect was extremely pretty, especially as some of the lamps had coloured glass in them.

I suddenly did not want to be with Edwin; let him look for the treasure on his own, I thought. I had seen Damien with Irene, and I was full of despair, bewilderment, the misery that inevitably follows great elation and happiness when one is in love.

I found myself near the Grotto of the Four Winds. I was wearing a shawl of the same colour as my dress, and I turned it up so that it covered my head as well as my shoulders, not wanting to catch a chill.

The moon lit the statues eerily. There was the South Wind, the sculpted woman who reminded me of Rose, the basket of flowers on her arm; the West Wind, with her corn-sheaf, facing towards Devon, the East Wind looking towards the Sun Grotto.

I sighed, staring out to sea; I heard a faint movement behind me, and I at once thought of Damien; he had come here to find me; he had escaped from Irene, we would have a few minutes alone together.

In a moment, he would call my name; I would turn and he would come to me and put his arms around me.

So I waited, and held my breath, hearing again the faint movement behind me; then I could bear the suspense no longer.

'Damien?' I whispered, as I turned.

The sixth sense that warned me of impending danger sprang to my defence with split-second timing. I was looking at the statue of the God of the North Wind, and even as I looked into the hard, craggy face, I saw it move forward, with a curious grinding movement. Its face seemed to rush swiftly towards mine; it was six foot high, and stood on a small marble plinth.

Instinctively, I sprang aside—only just in time; there was not a hair's-breadth between me and the falling statue as it crashed to the stone floor; its arm caught me a sharp glancing blow on the shoulder that sent me sprawling.

I screamed aloud with pain and terror. I saw a figure, no more than a moving shadow, melt into the bushes that grew near to the temple. The statue had broken in falling, and part of the arm that had struck me lay nearby, looking like a dismembered limb. I began to sob, as I got to my feet; my shoulder was throbbing, and I realised how near I had been to death.

At that moment, a figure appeared suddenly, beside the statue of the South Wind. It was Edwin. He stared down at the broken statue, and, as he lifted me to my feet, his hands were surprisingly gentle.

Chapter 7

I sat in the drawing-room at the House of the Four Winds, sipping the brandy that Edwin had insisted upon giving me; it was like fire and I choked on it, but gradually I stopped trembling so violently, and felt the blood move in my veins.

'That's better!' he said, with great satisfaction; he closed the door firmly against the sounds of revelry outside. Only a few people knew what had happened; we collected a handful of curious stares as Edwin helped me into the house and sent a servant in search of Rose.

My shoulder still throbbed where the falling statue had caught it; there was a mark on the skin that would be a bruise tomorrow. Edwin's fingers were firm and cool as they moved over the bare flesh of my shoulder.

'You've been lucky!' he said. 'A few more inches to the left and you would have received the full force of the falling statue; it could have killed you!'

I heard anger in his voice; Rose came into the room, looking horrified.

'Irene says that one of the statues in the Grotto of the Four Winds has fallen over!' she said. 'That is not possible! The statues have stood firm on their bases for years!'

'It didn't fall,' I said bleakly. 'Someone deliberately pushed it towards where I was standing.'

'Flora might have been killed!' Edwin told her grimly. His eyes were like flints.

Troubled, Rose stared down at me.

'I cannot believe it!' she whispered.

'I was wearing your pink dress,' I told her. 'I had a shawl over my head. I am as tall as you are, and it is quite dark outside.'

Suddenly, she put her hands over her face; the slender, exquisite white hands on which Jerome's jewelled tributes sparkled. It was only a brief surrender to horror; but when she took her hands away, her face was full of despair.

'It is absurd!' she cried. 'No one would wish to kill me! *Or* you!'

'You were my partner,' I said accusingly to Edwin. 'Where were you?'

'Looking for you, my dear Flora,' he retorted. 'You had conveniently lost me.'

'We cannot keep this from Jerome,' Rose said wearily. 'He will be furious!'

'Naturally.' Edwin's voice was dry. 'There are a good many people here tonight; many of them young and high-spirited. Yet, I would scarcely have thought that any of them had such a cruel taste in practical jokes. The only alternative is to suppose that someone wished you—or Flora—deliberate harm.'

'*Could* it not have been an accident?' she pleaded.

'Not unless there was an earthquake, my dear Rose,' he retorted, cynically.

'Jerome will be upset that the statue was broken, apart from anything else; he used to call himself the North Wind, and say that I was his South Wind.'

A reminiscent smile curved her lips briefly, though her eyes were unhappy.

'Did you see anyone near you?' Rose asked me.

'I heard someone move, behind me. I thought I saw someone running away, afterwards,' I told her.

'We were all out-of-doors,' Rose said. 'Even Jerome. We were both on the terrace, watching the others.'

I stood up determinedly, stilling the

queasiness in my stomach. I was prepared to believe anything except that someone had tried to kill me.

'I am ready to return to the party,' I said.

Edwin offered his arm.

'It is suppertime. Let us go.'

A splendid buffet had been laid on long tables in the supper room. The white cloths had been decorated with pink velvet ribbons and trails of greenery; a magnificent silver centrepiece held a huge cascade of crimson roses, with petals like silk.

Everyone crowded around me, wanting to know what had happened, and to enquire if I was recovered. I told them all that there seemed to have been some kind of an accident. Jerome did not put in an appearance, for which I was glad; Rose appeared, halfway through supper, and said that Jerome was exhausted, and resting in the library. She seemed worried about him.

Damien came up to me, demanding to know what had happened; I heard his sharp, angry intake of breath.

'Who did such a thing?' he asked ferociously.

186

'I don't know. I wish I did. I thought it was...you...coming...' my voice died away. He shook his head, a bitter expression on his face.

'Had *I* been there, such a thing would never have happened,' he told me curtly.

Irene came across the room to me; her eyes were bright and excited in her small, pale face.

'I hear you have had a most unpleasant experience, Miss Lindsay,' she said.

'Yes. I was fortunate to escape the more pressing attentions of the God of the North Wind,' I answered drily.

'How brave you are to make light of it! *I* should have been terrified!' She gave an affected little shiver as she smiled at her husband; it was a cold little smile.

'Where were *you*, Damien, when this happened?' she chided.

I saw a muscle twitch in his cheek.

'I was searching for you, Irene. We were partners in the treasure hunt, if you remember.'

'Ah! We were careless, to have lost one another in such a fashion,' she replied.

She murmured something about hoping I had recovered, and reminded Damien that the next dance was theirs.

I stood beside Edwin, under the crystal chandeliers; looking at the pretty women in their dresses like flowers, at the men, handsome in evening dress.

'What are you thinking about?' Edwin asked me.

'I am wondering if one of them tried to kill me,' I said.

'Do you find it a sobering reflection?'

'Very,' I replied drily.

He laughed, showing strong white teeth in his craggy face.

'You have courage, Flora,' he said admiringly.

Bella Careena sat on the end of my bed, wearing a long white nightgown; her feet were bare, and she was brushing her hair with long, slow strokes.

'It's the Curse of the Peacocks again,' she said. 'That's why the statue nearly fell on you.'

'Nonsense!' I said firmly.

'Oh yes, you always say that!' She looked angry. 'This monk who once lived here—his name was Alfrec de Bressard. He was supposed to be a good man and a hermit but he held black masses. You could hear screams and cries, over on

188

the mainland, and anyone landing here was never seen again. Well, *he* killed a peacock—the peacocks were wild, they always lived on the island and no one was supposed to touch them.'

'Where did you read this?'

'In the fifth grotto,' she said calmly.

She had my interest, at last; she knew it, and looked triumphant.

'You're not going to tell me where it is, are you?' I said resignedly.

'Of course not. I shall probably never tell anyone. It's my secret.'

'Edwin wants to find it,' I told her. 'Surely you'll tell him?'

She shook her head, lips pressed together. After a pause, she said:

'When Alfrec killed the Peacock, there was a great storm on the island; trees were blown down, and the waves came right up over the chapel. He was swept away and drowned. It's a bit like the legend of lost Atlantis, isn't it? Thousands of years ago, there was this beautiful place, Atlantis, full of people who became evil. So, one day, a great wave came out of nowhere, drowning the island and everyone in it. Sailors say you can hear the bells of Lost Atlantis, ringing sometimes, at the bottom of the seas. Lost Atlantis whispers, in a foam of bells, ice-cold and clear...'

Her voice died into silence; in spite of my belief that I should put a gentle rein on her imagination, I was intrigued by her words.

She smiled at me, an enigmatic smile as she slid from the bed. 'I hope you sleep well, Flora,' she murmured.

'I intend to; I have had enough excitement for one night.'

Unexpectedly, she kissed my cheek. It was the first spontaneous gesture she had made towards me.

'Goodnight, Bella,' I said. 'Have I at last convinced you that I have no intention of trying to persuade anyone to send you away to the mainland?'

'I think so,' she replied sedately.

In spite of my assurances that I was going to sleep well, I found it impossible to do so; I sighed wearily; got out of bed and went to the window.

Gently, I eased up the window, and leaned on the sill, listening intently; the night was still, but not quiet. It was full of small, soft rustlings and movements, as though the wild creatures had taken over and were going about their business undisturbed by humans; this was another life, an alien one; the one that Anne Churnock had cared for and protected.

The moon was high, printing black and silver shadows, sharp and clear, bathing the whole place in luminous light. Somewhere an owl hooted, and was answered by another owl. I thought of Damien, at Seawinds, and an unbearable loneliness ached within me. This was a night made for lovers.

I saw a movement in the grassy clearing below my window, and saw a figure step from a patch of deep shadow. I recognised him at once; tall, lean, craggy, the moonlight putting silver flecks in the dark hair. He stepped forward until he stood beneath my window, looking up at me, an impudent smile on his face, his eyes gleaming in the moonlight.

'Could I but sing, I would serenade you, Flora. I have a repertoire of French songs taught me by my grandmother, but they are slightly saucy, and not suited to a young lady's ears...'

'Hush!' I hissed furiously. 'You will wake the household.'

'I doubt it. Put on a wrapper and walk with me in the moonlight.'

'Certainly not!' I said, scandalised.

Edwin's soft laughter rippled up to me.

'Then put on a sedate dress, but don't fasten your hair; it becomes you better hanging loose over your shoulders. You look like the Queen of the Night, and I am reminded of a young lady who once threw her hairbrush at my feet, and then demanded it back again.'

In spite of my annoyance, my lips twitched. I stifled a laugh, and saw the pleasure in his face.

'I am making progress,' he called up softly. 'You no longer dislike me as much as you did.'

'You are ridiculous,' I scolded. 'Why are you out so late, when everyone else is in bed?'

'I have been to the Grotto of the Four Winds, with a lantern.'

'What on earth for?'

'I wished to examine the place, in view of that happened tonight,' he replied.

I leaned even farther out of the window.

'Did you find anything there?' I asked.

'Nothing that gives me reason to suppose the statue toppled from its plinth of its own accord. I tried the other statues. They stand firmly on their pedestals, though a good, hard push would send them over.'

'Do you have a list of suspects?' I asked, trying to hide my uneasiness.

'Alas, no. I shall consider the matter, as I walk by myself in the night. I am glad you are safe, my dear Flora—glad, in spite of your cold heart and indifference towards me!'

He laughed, swept a graceful bow, and blew me a kiss with his fingertips before he walked away.

Next day, Jerome sent for me; he looked grey and exhausted.

'I have heard what happened last night,' he said. 'I am deeply disturbed and very angry. I should have been told about it at the time.'

'Rose was anxious that you should not be distressed.'

'Distressed? Of course I am! Had I known of the incident yesterday evening, I would have questioned everyone present.'

'It would have spoiled the party,' I pointed out gently. 'Besides, no one would have owned up.'

'You could have been severely hurt!' he retorted.

'I wasn't, though; so please don't upset

yourself any longer. It is over. Perhaps it was one of the young men in the party from the mainland, playing a silly joke.'

'Well, it was certainly no one from the island, I am sure, not guest or servant. The whole episode has left an unpleasant memory,' he replied curtly.

'Then let it be wiped away,' I coaxed.

He shook his head, looking dissatisfied. Later that day two men came over from the mainland to take the statue away for repair. When they had gone, Rose and I walked down to the grotto; it didn't look the same without the proud God of the North Wind in his usual place.

'Jerome,' Rose said softly, tears in her eyes.

I looked at her enquiringly, and her smile was tremulous.

'Jerome, the God of the North Wind. There is a space where he should be. It seems like an omen!'

'Nonsense!' I told her firmly. 'The statue will be back as good as ever.'

'Oh, Flora!' she said, with a sigh, 'you *are* such a comfort!'

Later that morning, Rose asked me, looking hurt, why I did not wear the locket she had given me, and I told her.

She laughed gently.

'My dear, I think it would be delightful if you and Ruan entertained an affection for one another!'

'You cannot arrange such matters!' I protested.

She slid a hand through my arm as we walked together on the terrace.

'I'm not trying to arrange anything. I merely said it would be delightful.' She bit her lip, as though wondering whether to say anything more, and added:

'Forgive me, Flora. I don't wish to pry—but I cannot help noticing the looks that pass between you and Damien sometimes. You are—very much drawn towards him?'

'Yes,' I admitted reluctantly.

'I have seen, also, the way he looks at you. If there is mutual affection between you, then I beg you, Flora, to fight it with all your strength. It cannot bring you any happiness. Surely you must realise that? He is Irene's husband.'

In the afternoon, Bella and I went to the beach just below the house. I bathed there, for the first time in my life, and found the cold shock and the buoyancy of sea-water an exhilarating and delicious experience.

Bella swam with me, laughing at my efforts to float and to master the more complicated swimming strokes that she managed with such ease; she was like a porpoise in the water.

Afterwards, when we had dressed, we sat on the beach together. I was barefoot, my damp hair hanging about my shoulders. I had never enjoyed myself so much in all my life.

Bella did not like to sit still for very long; she ran down to the water's edge, letting the wavelets cream around her ankles. I leaned against a smooth slab of weathered rock and shut my eyes. I scarcely heard the sound of footsteps scrunching softly over the shingle bank behind me until a shadow fell between me and the sun.

I sat up at once, my eyes wide open. Damien was smiling down at me. Hastily, I tried to cover my ankles, but he shook his head, as he dropped down beside me.

'Don't do that, Flora; you have such pretty ankles,' he said.

Our shoulders touched; I thought my heart would break with the violence of its beating. I looked at Bella Careena, walking away from us, still at the water's edge.

'We have so little opportunity to talk together these days,' Damien said softly.

'We meet quite often,' I murmured.

'That is not what I meant, and you know it, Flora. I wish the summer was over; then Irene would return to London.'

'*I* shall go back to Bideford,' I replied.

'No, Flora,' he said softly. 'Stay with me here, when summer has gone. You will not find it dull, I assure you.' A strange smile curved his mouth. 'We shall do as we please, then, you and I; it will be—most entertaining. You will be mine, one day, Flora. Not Ruan's.'

'Why does everyone assume I am Ruan's property?' I demanded angrily.

'Because of the locket. It was most unwise of Rose to give it to you.'

'Do you hate Irene?' I asked slowly.

'No, my dear; hatred achieves nothing. Revenge may be born of hatred; but revenge must find and feed upon opportunity if it is to survive.'

'Revenge?' I echoed, looking at him in bewilderment. 'Do you then wish to be revenged upon her?'

'No!' He shook his head, his face enigmatic. 'I merely stated a fact. You and

I will keep our tryst, yet, at the Sun Grotto; on that day, I shall make you mine, Flora!'

'For a woman to lose her honour...' I began.

He laughed very softly; the light made a shining nimbus of his hair, reflected the fire in his eyes.

'The conventions mean nothing to those who desire one another, who long for one another, and wish to be one!' he told me gently.

He walked away, without another word; I bent my head to hide my tears.

I met Edwin in the library before dinner that evening; I had gone there in order to choose a book to while away night hours when sleep would not come.

He turned from the bookcase, a slim, leather bound volume in his hand. The lamplight made his craggy face look sharp and mocking, frosted the silver threads in his thick dark hair. His eyes rested on me approvingly.

'Ah, Flora Belle,' he said gaily. 'Are you in search of distraction? Can I recommend a little light reading?'

He held out the book he had been holding.

'Try this book, if you are interested in the island. It is full of stories and legends. Alas, it does not tell me where the fifth grotto may be found.'

I did not tell him that Bella knew the answer, I would sooner have bitten out my tongue.

'What is its importance to you, apart from the fact that your father created it?' I asked.

'It contains treasure, my dear,' he replied blandly.

'Golden ingots? Diamonds, rubies, emeralds?' My voice was as light as a snowflake.

'No. Treasure of a less substantial kind. Something that my father wrote. If ever I find the grotto, I may show it to you. It depends.'

'On what?'

'On you,' he said deliberately. 'You are a strange young woman. Wilful and capricious.'

'You don't really know me at all!' I retorted, furious at his cool assessment of me.

'True. Perhaps I never shall. It is for you to decide.'

His eyes met mine challengingly. I

199

shrugged and turned towards the bookcase.

'You have not asked me, recently, what the initial "P" stands for, on my hairbrush,' I said.

His reply infuriated me.

'I have decided to abandon the game; it is much too taxing in this hot weather.'

After dinner that evening, as I was returning to the cottage alone, I heard Rose talking to someone. I could not tell who it was; I was passing a small room at the end of the terrace, and the French doors were open to let in a little air, though the heavy curtains inside were pulled across.

Her voice was low and angry.

'*I* choose who shall come here, and I have decided that Flora shall stay here! It is her right, and my reasons are nothing to do with you. Remember, I am still Mistress of this island...'

I spent the rest of the evening in my room; puzzling over such a strange remark. There had been no answer, and though I had paused, I heard only the sharp slam of a door as though someone had left the room angrily.

It is her right; it is her right

It made no sense at all; I had no rights on this island, so far as I knew. I thought uneasily of the locket, the gifts she had given me, and wondered greatly.

Beneath all the golden loveliness of this island, the undercurrents ran dark and deep; people had secrets; whilst all the time their thoughts and their feelings were at variance with the facades they presented to one another.

It was a new experience for me; life had never been complex, nor had my relationships with other people caused me uneasiness until now.

Perhaps I should not have left Bideford at all, I reflected sadly; I should have burned my father's sketchbook, turned my back on my desire to see this place for myself; now its spell was upon me and the lives of its inhabitants were inextricably tangled with my life.

The boat went over to the mainland next morning, and returned with the mail. The little servant, Ann Jones, brought one letter to me as I was sitting in the garden checking lists for Rose.

The letter bore the Bideford postmark and Alexander Arkwright's writing sloped neatly across the envelope. I put the lists aside, and, with trembling fingers, I opened the envelope.

I read his covering note; my birth certificate was enclosed as requested, and he trusted that I was enjoying my stay on the island.

I spread the birth certificate out and studied it carefully. Date and place of birth, sex of child, father's name, name and maiden surname of mother.

Name and maiden surname of mother: written clearly in bold, beautiful copperplate. 'Lavinia Mary Lindsay (née Jessel).'

Chapter 8

I sat there for a long time, the certificate in my hand. I read the details several times; then I put it back in the envelope.

It was cool in the shade of the big tree, and there was no sound, save the soft sigh of the wind. Bella had gone for a fitting with the dressmaker; indoors, I heard little Anne Jones singing tunelessly to herself as she worked; and I remembered that Nanny Radford was in the house, too.

She was alone, in her small sitting-room, stitching at a torn dress of Bella Careena's; there was a pile of mending on the table beside her.

She put down her sewing, looking pleased to see me.

'Sit down then, Miss Lindsay. Too hot to be out of doors, on a day like this. It'll give you freckles, all that sun, and turn your skin to leather.'

'Nanny,' I said, loudly and clearly, 'tell me about the day that Edith Freemantle died. All that you can remember.'

She peered at me, surprised.

'What do you want to hear that old tale for?'

'I've only heard bits and pieces. I'm— curious.'

'Ah. Well, it was a terrible time and no mistake.' She sat back in her chair, letting the sewing drop into her lap. 'Never thought Miss Rose 'ud want to come and live here, after the accident, but I reckon Mr Jardine must have won her round. You know something? It was your father who took charge of everything, after it happened.'

'He didn't tell me that,' I said slowly.

'Maybe he thought the old story would upset you. Long before you were born, wasn't it? It was a day like this one; the sun like a furnace and not a bit of relief from the heat. I was nursemaid to Miss Edith, then, and a nastier, more spoiled child you've never come across. She was an orphan and heiress to a lot of money. Mr Brandon, Miss Rose's father, was her legal guardian. Mean? Huh!' Nanny made a gesture of utter contempt, and continued:

'As for Mrs Brandon, she was a poor creature, and no mistake. Always ailing, or whining about something. What a household it was, and the only ray of sunshine was Miss Rose. Different, *she* was; had a nice nature. The governess, Miss Jessel—Vinnie, as she was called—*she* found Edith a right handful, poor soul. Always making trouble for the servants, that child was.'

'Did *you* like Miss Jessel?' I asked, watching her closely.

'Oh yes. Quiet little creature, always friendly and anxious to please, and tried to do her best for Edith, but she was no match for the child; and Mr Brandon didn't have time for Vinnie, neither. Took it out on her whenever he was in the mood; treated her like a servant; he was always saying a governess thought herself a cut above a servant and gave herself airs; and there was Mrs Brandon, expecting her to be a lady's maid, as well; fetch this, carry that, do that...ah, poor soul, she had a wretched life of it!'

I bowed my head, feeling the tears sting my eyelids; Nanny glanced curiously at me.

'Anything wrong, Miss Lindsay?'

'The heat,' I lied.

'Just like it was then. The picnic on the island was Miss Rose's idea. Mr Jerome owned the place, then, and he let them all come and go as they pleased. He let Mr Lindsay go there sketching, too.

'Next to sketching, he liked sailing. A nice man he was, too; *very* fond of Miss Rose, and she was fond of him. *Everyone* liked Miss Rose.'

Nanny fell silent, remembering, no doubt.

'The day of the picnic...' I prompted.

'Well, poor Miss Jessel wasn't well, and half out of her mind with worry, because Mr Brandon had given her notice...he had a cousin coming to live with them who could look after Edith's lessons. Miss Jessel hadn't nowhere to go, and she said jobs like hers weren't easy to come by; she told me so, that morning. She looked sick enough to be in bed, I told her, not to be going out in the sun...

'I was down at the Fortune; Mrs Finney, who was living there then, was a friend of mine. I saw Mr Lindsay come back from a sail and tie the boat up; I remember thinking how hot and bothered he looked, had to use the oars, because there wasn't no wind, not a drop, and Mrs Finney called out to him to come and have a cool drink...he said he'd be glad to...he looked all in, I remember...

'We were all sitting in the window of the Fortune when we saw the boat coming back from the island, with Abel Carter and his brother rowing like mad, and something up, you could tell. When the boat came in, there was Miss Rose, in a terrible state, and they had Edith's body in the boat—that gave me a right turn—and poor Miss Jessel lying in the bottom, moaning and crying and saying things that didn't make sense and every few minutes she'd go right off again, and then she'd come to...*dreadful* it was. Miss Rose was hysterical and your father took charge of everything, quietened her down, got poor Miss Jessel into the Fortune, sent for Mr Brandon and the doctor, and tried to comfort Miss Rose and find out what had happened.

'Mr Brandon wouldn't have Miss Jessel back at the house when he heard what had happened. I reckon that was cruel of him; still, I heard afterwards she'd been sent to be nursed privately somewhere, I suppose he reckoned he could afford *that*.'

Nanny's voice was sour with sudden cynicism. I thought of the blazing heat of a sweltering afternoon, a dead child and a half-conscious woman, and Rose in a state of shock, in a boat gliding through the summer seas, away from the island. I shivered, and felt goose prickles along my arm, as though I had been there, part of the dreadful happenings.

'Well, it all came out afterwards,' Nanny said. 'Miss Rose had been sitting near some ruins, sketching, and Miss Jessel had been on the beach looking after Edith. Miss Rose said she didn't know anything was wrong, she heard a couple of screams and thought it was the peacocks; they were half-wild; nasty birds they are. Miss Rose said when she had finished sketching she started off for the beach, and found the governess lying under a tree, moaning and crying and saying she'd lost Edith. She had a great lump on her forehead and said she'd had a fall; then poor Miss Rose found the child, lying on the rocks, with her skull fractured, and the tide coming in.'

I felt dreadfully sick; my head was swimming, and nausea filled me. I could see it clearly, the waves lapping at the spreadeagled figure of the child who had fallen down to the beach.

'Edith must have fell awkward-like,'

Nanny said, shaking her head. ' 'Tain't all that much of a drop, they said, but she hit the rocks.'

'Where were the boatmen?' I asked.

'Oh, *them* two!' Nanny said, with great scorn. 'Fast asleep, near the jetty; waiting to row the party back, they said, and just dozed off... Well, there 'twas. The curse of the island, Miss Bella calls it. Carelessness, *I* say. If you're looking after a handful like Edith, you can't afford to let up, not for a minute. I spoke up for Miss Jessel; said she hadn't been right when she left the house, she'd looked ill to me. All I got for my pains was being told to mind my own business by Mr Brandon. It was all kept very quiet, Miss Jessel got the blame, and the Brandons didn't want any fuss made. It did *him* a lot of good. My word, didn't his style of living change after that! He neglected the church; in the end he gave it up for good. Rich? *He* had money to spare, all right, with Edith Freemantle dead.'

'Where was he, that afternoon?'

Nanny grinned wickedly at me, showing yellow teeth.

'Now, Miss Lindsay, you're not thinking wrong things, I hope? He was in his study,

209

preparing his sermon, and there were plenty to prove it; and Mrs Brandon was lying down with one of her migraines; the doctor called to see her, there was a couple of the maids in the house. Mr Jerome had gone to Dorchester; Sir Marcus was busy working on some sketches he'd made for the gardens. Young Master Edwin was away in the fields somewhere; you know what boys are. Master Damien went sailing; he was staying with Mr Jerome, like he often did.'

'What happened to Miss Jessel after she left the nursing home?' I asked.

Nanny shook her head and looked blank.

'Never heard nothing more about her. Miss Rose used to worry a lot, I know. Said she had been treated shocking. Maybe she could tell you.'

Miss Rose used to worry a lot. She would have been glad, I thought, that poor little Miss Jessel had married Mr Richard Lindsay, even though she had been second-best then, for my father had loved the woman Marcus Trehearne married. I knew, now, the identity of the woman who had visited us at Bideford on the days when my father took me out.

Little Lavina Jessel had covered up her

tracks very well; made sure that her daughter knew nothing of the past; but she was *not* to blame, I thought angrily! What happened was not her fault! Wilfrid Brandon used her cruelly and then disposed of her, hushing up the incident for fear a scandal would affect his inheritance. Anger burned within me, fiercer than the sun's heat; anger against Edith. Against Wilfrid.

Rose had been troubled and unhappy, knowing there had been injustice done; she had wanted to make amends, and found a way of doing so when she believed I had been left without means following the death of my father.

It explained so much; yet I had a feeling that only half of the jigsaw puzzle was complete.

'Sure you're feeling quite well, Miss Lindsay? You *do* look pale. I should go and lie down if I were you,' Nanny said.

I rose stiffly to my feet.

'Thank you,' I said. 'I will.'

I drew the curtains against the sun; my head throbbed, and I lived every moment of that afternoon as my mother must have lived it, ill, unhappy, desperate. No wonder she had shown such compassion for the woman who had been *my* governess!

I kept remembering how I had felt the day I had first gone to the Shell Grotto. I recalled the cold prickling of my skin, the throbbing of my head, my intense revulsion for the place. I wished that my mother had talked to me of what happened, then. She must have suffered a severe nervous breakdown afterwards—and no one had cared, except my father—and Rose.

Jerome and Rose knew what had happened that day; Damien and Edwin also knew the tragic events that took place on the island; but did any of them, except Rose, know I was Vinnie's daughter?

Jerome would certainly know, I reasoned; Rose would not have kept any knowledge from the man she loved so much. Did Edwin and Damien also know? Or Ruan—had he been told about me?

The taking of the photograph from my locket now had a new significance. It was an old photograph; anyone who had known Lavinia Jessel would recognise her; and *I* had announced to everyone that the picture in the locket was that of my mother.

The more I thought about it, the more

confused I became. The first sharp shock had dulled into an ache of misery for my mother.

I decided to say nothing to Rose yet concerning my discovery.

On my way from the cottage to have lunch at the House of the Four Winds, I met Ruan.

'Hello, Flora! You look very cool and charming.' His smile was suddenly wicked. 'I am glad to see you are wearing the family heirloom; mama *will* be pleased.'

'There's nothing special in acknowledging your mother's kindness by wearing her gift,' I retorted.

'Ah, dear Flora, you disappoint me!' he murmured teasingly. 'Mama would look most favourably upon a romantic attachment between us!'

'*I* have not been consulted in the matter!' I replied, tossing my head.

'But you *do* like me, don't you?'

'Yes,' I said.

'I like *you*; now that's a good beginning, I think.'

I looked into the candid, laughing eyes; here was a good-looking man with a great deal of charm, I thought. It would be easy, perhaps, to fall in love with him were it not for Damien.

'You are a tease,' I told him lightly.

'I am not teasing, I assure you,' he said, trying to look solemn.

I was thrown into a sudden panic. Too much was happening to me, all at once. I had not yet recovered from the shock of discovering the identity of my mother.

His voice was playful; his smile was still teasing, but there was no laughter in his eyes.

During lunch, I watched Rose carefully; only a very close observer would have seen the look of strain on her face. Only I knew the cause; every hour, every day was precious to her; each beat of the clock brought her nearer to the time when Jerome would no longer be with her, and I could guess what agony she suffered because of that knowledge. The long, hot summer was taking what little strength he had left. There were questions I wanted to ask; but I had to be discreet.

I spoke to Damien; I found an opening for the subject when I walked over to Seawinds that afternoon with a message from Rose to Irene.

I saw him along the path that led from the Shell Grotto; I waited, and when he saw me waiting, he came quickly towards me, delight in his face; impetuously, he caught me in his arms beneath the shade of the tree, holding me close, kissing my eyelids, my cheeks, my mouth, until I pulled away, gasping for breath.

'Still so timid?' he murmured, eyebrows raised. 'One day, Flora, I will teach you the meaning of passion. Don't tell me that such a day will never come, for I will not listen to you. It *will* come, Flora; it will!'

'I shall never consent to becoming your mistress,' I told him firmly.

He smiled, and changed the subject.

'Where are you going?' he asked.

'To Seawinds.'

'So am I; we'll walk together. I have been down to the beach, below the Shell Grotto. It is the most secluded of all the beaches. I like to swim from there.'

'Neptune's Bay? That is where Edith fell to her death.'

'My dear Flora, I am not superstitious,' he said, with a touch of sharpness. 'It happened a quarter of a century ago. People would have forgotten about it by

215

now, if only Bella didn't keep the story alive.'

'I doubt if the governess ever forgot what happened that day,' I pointed out. 'Did you know her?'

'Scarcely at all; she was a quiet, nondescript little creature, engaged to look after Edith Freemantle and totally unfitted for the task. *I* kept out of Edith's way. The day she was killed I was sailing along the coast and didn't return until evening.'

His voice warned me not to pursue the subject; clearly, he found the memory distasteful. It was obvious that *he* did not know Vinnie was my mother.

Irene was walking in the grounds of Seawinds when we arrived; she looked like a ghost of summer in her white, floating dress, her face pale beneath her shady hat.

I gave her the message, anxious to be away; her eyes seemed to pierce right through me. When she smiled, it was a travesty of a smile, merely a weary lifting of the corners of her mouth as though she found life an unpalatable jest.

'I know you think you are in love with Damien,' she said calmly, as though she was giving the day's orders to the housekeeper. 'He pretends to love you; he does *not*. He is incapable of love. When he has had you, used you and done with you, he will forget that you ever existed.'

I said nothing, because I did not know what to say. The smile became contemptuous; she put out a slender, waxen-looking finger and touched the locket at my throat.

'You should settle for Ruan,' she said scathingly. 'What a prize for a penniless governess! For that is all you are: a penniless governess!'

The irony of her description struck me so forcibly that I hated her, for a moment; the hatred passed, to be replaced by something curiously like pity.

'You are a fortune hunter,' she added. 'Ruan's mama dotes on you; I cannot think why, but she seems to think you would make Ruan an excellent wife. Ruan would be an easy conquest for you, wouldn't he? A wealthy husband—and *my* husband at a discreet distance, ready to rescue you from the boredom you will feel sooner or later—because Ruan is a mere boy; and you, Flora Lindsay, will demand a man, with full-blooded passions...'

'You have my word that I have not been your husband's mistress, nor do I intend to be,' I replied.

'Liar!' she said venomously.

'Believe what you choose,' I said; I walked away and left her, resisting the temptation to look back.

Well, I would make sure there was no more guilt on my part; I would avoid Damien. If I did not do so, I would be drawn down into a whirlpool of emotions that would engulf me.

The feeling grew within me that the golden days were ending; that we were all moving helplessly towards some terrible and tragic climax. I said nothing to Rose; she had burdens enough as it was. There were times when she seemed exhausted, completely drained of energy; yet her smile never faltered; her love for Jerome shone clearly through all that she said and did.

So many times, the words were on the tip of my tongue: *I know I am Vinnie's daughter.*

Perhaps I should tell Jerome, I thought; still I hesitated. I had a great desire to know all about the affair of Edith Freemantle; and the small thought nagged, like a toothache in my mind, that something was still withheld from me, some knowledge still denied me.

Often, when I walked about the island, I was certain that I was followed; but I could not find out who followed me, I was never quick enough to see who walked only a short distance from me; the island was a perfect place for anyone bent on a game of stalking.

Sometimes Bella walked with me; but lately she had taken to going off on her own a great deal. She was writing her own history of the island, she said, and took a large exercise book and pencil with her, hiding away in one of many secret places that only she knew.

I was glad to be alone, although my thoughts were poor company; so, walking in the green coolness of the trees on a scorching afternoon, I came to the end of the little grove of trees leading to the niche where the Cupid stood.

On the flat-roofed rock that made a natural seat at the feet of Cupid, Jerome and Irene were sitting together.

His arms were around her, her head was on his shoulder. I could not clearly see the expression on Jerome's face, but he stroked her hair gently, and spoke softly to her.

Stunned, I stood behind a concealing tree, watching them; after a few moments, Irene lifted her head and looked at Jerome. Her face was streaked with tears; I heard her voice, clear and accusing.

'Flora is having an affair with Damien! You must have seen that, Jerome! You must have seen how they look at one another!'

I did not hear his reply, but I saw him shake his head; and the words she flung back to him were angry.

'You are Master here, Jerome! You can send her away. I tell you it is true, and I will not tolerate it...'

Again he spoke quietly to her. She dabbed at her cheeks with a scrap of lace, and stood up, jerking away angrily from his protective embrace, as she twitched her skirts into place.

I turned and fled.

I sat in my room at the cottage, trying to read and unable to concentrate. I felt cold, in spite of the heat of the day; my hands were shaking, my thoughts would not be quiet.

My love for Damien would bring disaster

upon us both if I did not leave the island soon, I realised.

The time had come for me to approach both Rose and Jerome, tell them the truth about myself, and admit to having witnessed the scene in the woods.

The following afternoon I came upon Rose and Jerome in the conservatory taking tea together. They sat side by side, on chairs of wrought iron, and the tea tray, with its silver appointments, was set in front of them on a low table. Rose looked very beautiful in a pale dress the colour of hyacinths that set off her lovely eyes and rich, wheat-coloured hair to perfection; one slender, white hand with its jewelled fingers held Jerome's hand, as he sat beside her, looking pale and tired, but relaxed.

They looked up and smiled when they saw me; Jerome got to his feet, and told me to summon a servant to bring fresh tea.

He glanced at the heavy gold locket I wore, and said mildly:

'I hear there has been speculation because my wife gave you a family heirloom. Only tradition says it is destined for a Jardine bride. You must make up your own mind, Flora; as I did. As Rose did.'

I met his penetrating look calmly.

'I like Ruan very much,' I said quietly. 'I think he is a fine young man; I have no feelings other than those of warm friendliness towards him.' I turned to Rose. 'Does that disappoint you?' I asked frankly.

'Only a little,' she admitted, with a smile. 'It would be lovely to have you as a daughter-in-law, Flora; but, as Jerome says, we all make up our own minds on such matters. When Ruan marries, there will be other jewels to hand down to his bride. The locket was an especial gift to you—from me.'

As soon as the fresh tea had been brought, Jerome said briskly:

'Now, Flora; what troubles you?'

'I must leave here soon,' I said as calmly as I could.

'*Leave?*' Rose looked incredulous. 'Why, Flora? *Why?* Are you not happy with us?'

I drew a deep breath; it was going to be far more difficult to tell them about Damien than to tell them I knew my mother's identity, I realised.

So I told Jerome of the scene I had witnessed in the woods between him and Irene. I saw Rose grow even more pale, so that her face was devoid of all colour, and she glanced sharply at Jerome, who sat impassively.

Rose looked at me; there were tears in her eyes, and her voice was so soft that I scarcely heard the words.

'It isn't true, is it, Flora?' she begged piteously.

'It *is* true that I have very strong feelings for Damien,' I said, staring down at my hands clasped, trembling, in my lap. 'He also entertains strong feelings for me. I have behaved foolishly and indiscreetly, but I have not misconducted myself in the way Irene believes. I feel that it is best for me to return to Bideford, where I shall be out of touch with him, and learn to forget him.'

Forget him? Never, I thought! I looked up and saw the terrible anguish in Rose's face.

'My dear Flora, you have no idea how unhappy I am to know that this situation has arisen,' Jerome said sadly.

'You *do* believe that I have not misconducted myself with Damien? That there have been no more than words and kisses between us—even though that, in itself, is a matter for shame on my part?' I whispered.

'Yes, I believe you. Irene is overwrought; Damien plans to leave her.'

'If her marriage has been so unhappy, surely that will please her?' I replied.

'You must surely be aware of the social stigma a woman suffers when her husband leaves her,' Jerome pointed out.

Rose lifted her head; I saw both fury and fear in her face.

'He shall not stay here?' she whispered. 'He shall *not!*'

'He is the owner of Seawinds,' Jerome reminded her quietly. 'Whatever we may feel about his conduct towards Flora, my dearest, we cannot compel him to leave the island.'

'Exactly,' I said briskly. 'It is best that *I* should leave. I have seen the island; I have been happy here, and shall take away pleasant memories with me. There is one more thing that I must tell you. I requested my solicitor to send my birth certificate, and he did so. I know that I am Lavinia Jessel's daughter.'

Rose was the first to break the silence. She asked, very quietly:

'What made you suspect the truth?'

'Your—great affection for me. I *wondered*, greatly; then it occurred to me that

224

my mother had always been reticent about her youth.'

'She did not want you to know,' Jerome said heavily. 'She went to great lengths to keep it from you because she was a proud and sensitive woman. There was an account of the accident in the newspapers, and when Wilfrid Brandon made it clear to everyone that he blamed her entirely for what happened, she suffered agonies of mind.'

'My father was a hypocrite,' Rose said, with intense bitterness. 'Poor, poor Vinnie!' She bent her head, crying softly. 'I wanted so much to make it up to her. I traced her to the nursing home. Richard—your father, Flora—was shocked and distressed about it all; he showed her great compassion and understanding.'

'Did he marry her from pity?' I asked.

'No.' The tears were still falling, and I saw the almost iron grip of Jerome's fingers on hers. 'The first woman in your father's life was Sara Trehearne, who married Edwin's father. Caring for your mother healed the wound for Richard.'

'When Richard and your mother were married in Bristol, I attended the ceremony, at your father's request,' Jerome told me. 'Rose kept in touch with your mother; she even went to visit her occasionally.'

I smiled tiredly.

'I knew. She wouldn't let us meet, would she, Rose? In case I discovered the truth. If only she had told me; I would have understood.'

'Would you?' Jerome asked drily. 'You were only fourteen when she died. She was very happy with your father. She said her marriage had brought her contentment, peace of mind and a beloved daughter. She needed nothing more.'

I felt a tightness within my throat, a heavy weight behind my eyelids; I said gently to Rose:

'You were kind to my mother; for that, you have my gratitude, always.'

She was tensed; taut and nervous, as though she held on to her self-control with immense difficulty.

'If I had stayed with Vinnie, that day, the accident would not have happened,' she whispered forlornly.

'My mother would not wish you to blame yourself,' I assured her.

She smiled; a tired little smile that ended on a sigh.

'She told me, often, that I should not

feel guilty; but if *only* I had seen that Vinnie was not fit to look after Edith,' she answered sadly.

'It is all over. I'm glad I know the truth about my mother,' I told her. 'Does anyone else know it?'

Out of the small silence, Jerome said quietly:

'Yes. Edwin. His father was always anxious to patch up the old quarrel with your father, and wrote, many years ago. The letter was not answered. He was worried, and had some enquiries made, as a result of which he discovered the truth. He told Edwin; but Edwin is aware that your mother wished you to remain in ignorance, and he would never betray her.'

So Damien did not know. Nor Irene. Nor Bella and Ruan. Well, none of it was important, now; I had one last task to fulfil.

'You thought I was in need of employment, when my father died,' I said.

'Yes,' answered Rose, 'though your home seemed comfortable enough to me, I knew nothing of your father's finances, nor did I ever expect your mother to discuss them with me. I assumed you were left without means when your father died. It is not an unusual situation.'

'I have not been honest with you,' I said frankly. 'My father was a rich man—I did not know the extent of his wealth until his death. You assumed I was penniless, and I did not correct the mistake because I wanted to come here on my own merits, not as an heiress. It was cheating, though; you pay me a generous wage, which I must return.'

For the first time that afternoon, Jerome really smiled.

'My dear child, I am delighted to know you are provided for; as for your wages, you have earned them. Keep them!'

'Dear Flora, I do not want you to leave here,' Rose said, still looking unhappy.

'It is for the best,' I insisted firmly.

'Stay a little longer,' she urged. 'A week or two.'

I bent my head, lost; ashamed of my weakness.

'Another two weeks, then,' I whispered, vowing not to be alone with Damien.

'Never let the past make you unhappy,' Jerome told me. 'Your mother put the past behind her and found happiness; as, one day, you will.'

'I shall never marry,' I told him.

'Why on earth not?'

'Because I shall be wooed for my fortune, not for my face,' I replied.

'You underestimate yourself, dear Flora,' Rose told me.

The events of the day had exhausted me; I pleaded a headache and asked to be excused from putting in an appearance at dinner. I went to the cottage and Anne brought a supper-tray to my room.

Bella Careena came to see me, with some eau-de-cologne; she looked concerned and I realised how much I was going to miss her; from uncertain beginnings, we were progressing towards a good friendship, and I hoped Rose would not tell her daughter, until the last possible moment, that I was leaving the island.

'Mama says you are not feeling well,' said Bella, patting cologne on to my throbbing temples.

'It's the heat,' I said, with a smile.

'I should go to bed, if I were you,' she said briskly, as though I was the child, and she was the adult. 'You'll feel better in the morning.'

I smiled at her, wished her goodnight, and decided to take her advice; but I could not sleep, and tossed in my bed most of the night.

I didn't want any breakfast, though I made a pretence of eating some, under the watchful eyes of Bella and Nanny Radford. Afterwards, I went for a walk to the folly.

I went into the church and sat there, staring up at the stained glass window; I could find no peace, and I knew it was my own fault. I came out into the sunshine again, and read the lovely inscription on the tomb of Ann Churnock.

I didn't want to return either to the House of the Four Winds or to the cottage. The desire to be out-of-doors with my thoughts had never been so strong. I walked on past the cottage, past the house, and came to the clearing where the folly stood.

The door was open; a figure stood at the top, staring at the tall firs that reached to meet the sky; when he saw me, he leaned over the stone parapet and cupped his hands around his mouth.

'Come up, Flora! Come and see what I see!'

'No!' I called back.

'Ah, I forgot; you dislike heights; but you will be safe with me.'

The voice was teasing, tantalising; Edwin was leaning over, beckoning, and I was tired of my own company.

It wasn't such a long climb, after all; I took it slowly, refusing to think about the height of the tower. I thought about other things; preparations for Ruan's celebrations, already far advanced. The flowers planned, the caterers' menu approved, dust sheets being taken from furniture in rooms not used, the whirr of a sewing machine as Miss Hyams worked against the clock; and I would not be here to see any of it.

Edwin waited at the top, an unfathomable expression in his eyes.

'Well done, Flora. I said you had courage!'

'What is it you see from here?' I asked impatiently.

'Look!' he said, standing close to me, and pointing upwards. 'Look at the tip of that fir. What do *you* see?'

'Only a bird,' I told him, disappointed.

'A sparrowhawk; it is not every day that one sees a sparrowhawk.'

I looked again; it was a large bird,

sitting motionless against the blue sky; slowly it turned its head in our direction, and I saw the bright, searching eyes, the cruelly curved beak. There was something repellent about it, and I shivered.

'There is a nest of young sparrowhawks in the tree,' Edwin told me. 'The father hunts for food, and carries it back in his claws.'

'I don't like birds of prey,' I told him.

'In their way, they are fascinating, Flora. They wait and they watch, and nothing deflects them from that waiting and watching; when they are ready, they swoop, silently, on their prey.'

'Some defenceless bird or mouse, I suppose.'

'That is nature; nature is cruel.'

I felt sick; and suddenly giddy. The panorama of the island was spread around me, like a great carpet; trees, buildings, church tower, the two houses and Bella Careena's cottage, the blue girdle of water encircling it all and the green hump of the mainland.

Edwin put an arm about my shoulders, gripping me so tightly that I could not move away. Behind me was the winding stair; in front of me, a long drop to the ground. The parapet was only waist-high; I was afraid, and fought it back. I would not let Edwin Trehearne see fear in my face.

'Isn't it a beautiful sight?' he murmured.

'Yes,' I said quietly.

'From here, you can see it all, the whole island, the people coming and going about their business. You must never be afraid of heights—or depths, Flora. The view from the heights is always wonderful; as for the depths, they teach us to climb up to the sun.'

'Are you trying to tell me something?' I asked him.

'Perhaps. A riddle for you to read. Are you bored? Shall I entertain you instead with stories of the escapades of my French grandmother, who outwitted her enemies and donned a dozen different disguises along the route of her escape to England? Perhaps this is no time for frivolous tales. You look sad, Flora Belle!'

I looked up into the face so near my own; there was no mockery in it, though his brown eyes were alert and watchful.

'You know who I am,' I said.

'Indeed I do. You are Miss Flora P Lindsay, who does not intend to satisfy my curiosity about her middle name. You are a stubborn, self-willed, courageous, unpredictable young woman, who is just beginning to discover what life is all about.'

'That isn't what I meant. You know that I am Lavinia Jessel's daughter.'

'Yes,' he said calmly. 'How did *you* come upon the truth?'

I told him; he listened in silence. Finally, he said:

'I was a boy of thirteen when it happened, Flora. I didn't know your mother well, but I met her a few times, and I felt sorry for her. It was natural that she should want you to be kept in ignorance about the events of that terrible day. Remember, the knowledge was kept from you for the best of reasons. Now you know; and it is in the way you accept such things that you either enrich or impoverish your life.'

'I know little enough about life, yet,' I admitted wryly.

'True. You are now being given the opportunity to learn. Before you know life, you must know yourself; and your heart. You must first learn to separate love from mere infatuation.'

'You think I am merely infatuated with Damien, don't you?' I cried bitterly.

'I *know* you are. No one can help you; it is a jungle through which you must hack your own way.'

'Oh wise Edwin, who has never felt the need of a woman's love!' I retorted bitterly.

'Who told you that?' His voice was dangerously quiet.

'Ruan. He says you have never needed a wife.'

'That is true. I have not been celibate, like a monk, Flora.' His voice was still soft. 'I have had mistresses; enjoyed women's bodies as well as their minds, but never lied to them with pretences of love, and never treated them badly.'

'And never truly loved?' I cried triumphantly.

'You are wrong, you know; I love *you*. Much good will it do me. Have your victory, Flora!' His voice was suddenly savage. 'I shall not speak of this again. Enjoy Damien whilst you may; he reminds me of the sparrowhawk, who watches and waits, with infinite patience, for the right moment to swoop on his prey!'

Angrily, I pulled free of his encircling arm. He did not love me; he mocked me.

He was a stranger; hard, ice-cold. He went ahead of me down the stairs, and I followed, my legs trembling. I felt utterly exhausted.

In spite of my vow not to be alone with Damien, there came a time, two days later, when I could not avoid him. It was just before dinner, at Four Winds; he was alone in the drawing-room when I arrived, standing with his back to the room, hands clasped behind him, as he stared out into the velvet night.

My heart beat fast; the blood thundered in my pulses, as he turned and smiled at me.

'*Flora!*' He came across, holding out his hands; when I stood helpless before him, not attempting to touch those outstretched hands, he frowned and said softly:

'You have been avoiding me; why?'

'You know why,' I stammered. 'To meet will only make an impossible marriage situation worse.'

'Someone has been talking to you,' he said shrewdly, his eyes narrowing. 'Rose, perhaps?'

I shook my head, saying nothing. I thought he looked like one of the statues

236

in the Temple of the Four Winds come to life. I knew that if he commanded me to come away with him, I would have gone to the edge of the world and beyond.

His smile was warm and slow; it hinted at possibilities I dared not consider, at a future I could not contemplate.

'Only be patient,' he said slowly. 'Be patient and trust me.'

'I am going away,' I told him, with all the strength I could muster.

'When?'

'In a little while. It is best,' I said.

'It is nonsense!' he retorted. 'Stay for Ruan's coming-of-age celebrations! *Then* we shall see if you want to leave the island!'

'I don't understand,' I stammered.

'You will understand everything, one day.' Gently, he stroked my cheek with a fingertip, adding:

'I tell you, Flora, that soon, Irene will have no part in our lives. Only be patient for a little while longer. Bella Careena is about to add one more chapter to its strange history, and I want you to be there to see it!'

Chapter 9

Rose said that if she had decided to stay with Vinnie on that fateful day, Edith might not have died; had she done so, it is probable that I would never have come to the island, at all. Fate hangs by very slender threads; and had I not got up earlier than usual, a couple of days after my strange conversation with Damien, then the ending to my own story might well have been different.

The night had been clammy; the east was still pearl grey when I arose from my bed, dressed, and decided I needed to walk in the fresh air, before anyone was about.

I let myself quietly out of the house; it did not much matter which direction I took: north, east, south or west. I walked aimlessly for a little while, and when I saw Damien, he was ahead of me, beyond the trees that shielded me, walking due east in the direction of the Sun Grotto.

I cannot say what utter madness possessed me, then, making me follow him. I was lost to all thoughts of modesty or dignity; I forgot my vow I had made to myself. I only knew that I wanted to be alone with him, for one last time. Such was the strength of my feelings for him that I cared for nothing except my own desires.

I wondered if he went alone to the Sun Grotto every morning, hoping that I would join him; the thought made my heart leap. I decided I would follow him, surprise him, sit and talk with him awhile; I tried to imagine his delight when he saw me...

Perhaps, in my heart, I believed in the promise he had made that Irene would not always come between us, that there would be happiness in the future; though how he could hope to keep such a promise, I did not know...

I knew that I *had* to talk to him; now, before I left the island for ever.

The trees thinned out as he reached the little headland that led to the Grotto. Now there were only stunted bushes, growing low to the ground, crouched against the skyline.

I thought how splendid Damien looked;

he was casually dressed in silk shirt, riding breeches and boots. I hugged to myself the thought of creeping up to surprise him, calling his name softly, seeing him turn.

He walked to the tip of the little headland, and then dropped down slightly on to the beach below. Soundlessly, I sped along the sandy little path between the furze and bushes, until I was right above him.

I looked down on a tall, well-built figure, a head of bright curls; Damien sat on a flat slab of rock near the grotto entrance, looking relaxed, as he stared out to sea. The sun was not yet up, the sea was like wrinkled grey silk; the tide was going out, and showed the wet, ribbed sand, where a couple of seagulls strutted, looking for food.

I knew a moment of pure delight; a delicious, feminine sense of power in watching whilst he remained unaware of my presence.

As I edged closer to the very edge of the low cliff, and drew breath to call his name, I saw his head jerk sharply to the right, as though he had seen someone.

He rose to his feet; still with a leisurely air, as though he had all the time in the world, and turned towards the figure walking along the wet sand at the water's edge, towards him.

I recognised her at once; it was Rose.

She walked slowly, as though she was very tired; her golden hair fell loosely about her face; she wore a plain, dark dress and her shoulders drooped. She was quite unlike the regal figure who had stood beside her husband on the terrace of the House of the Four Winds, welcoming me...

Damien laughed and held out his arms to her; crouched against the bushes, I stared at her in utter disbelief.

Rose stopped dead, just out of reach of his arms; she glanced at him scornfully.

'Have you no welcome for me, dear heart?' he mocked softly.

'None,' she said flatly. 'I asked you to meet me here because it is the one place where there is no possibility of our being overheard. Unless, of course, you have an assignment with Flora?'

His teeth showed white in his handsome face; he threw back his head and laughed.

'Flora? She is too timid to turn her desires into reality!' he retorted. 'She loves me to distraction, my dear Rose, but fears both herself and the conventions!'

'She is merely infatuated with you, though she does not know it, yet,' Rose retorted.

'You are wrong, Rose. She has a great and consuming passion for me. It would be easy to seduce her, but the time has not yet come. When that time does come, it will be an enjoyable experience, for us both. I find her desirable. A woman of spirit. Very like you, my love. Shall we go into the grotto to discuss whatever it is you are so anxious to talk to me about? *Shall* we, Rose? And then make love there, as we did all those years ago?'

'You are vile!' she choked. 'You spoiled the grotto for me!'

'You did not think so, then. You were ardent and willing, on the day you conceived Ruan!' he jibed.

'With your son in my womb, I knew I hated you!' she retorted fiercely, pushing back the bands of hair from her face. 'The spell you had over me was broken, then! Would to God I had never let you know he *was* your son! At least he does not resemble you in any way! How I hate you still!'

'Pity and hatred are both akin to love!'

he replied, laughing.

'Don't harm Flora, please,' she said quietly.

'Ah! If I did, you would bear double guilt, wouldn't you? I know very well whose daughter she is, Rose. It was *I* who found the locket, and recognised the photograph.'

'Was it you, also, who damaged it and threw it into the grotto?' she demanded angrily.

'What else did you expect me to do? Return it to her? I was too furious, Rose. Furious that you should have brought Vinnie's daughter here. It was indiscreet of you; if she asks too many questions, you might decide, in your folly, to answer them; and that would never do.'

I saw a peculiar expression cross her face, gone in an instant. I stayed immobile, my body numb, my mind alive, raging in agony, disbelief and horror...

'Now. Why did you ask me to meet you here today?' he demanded curtly.

I saw her steady herself with an effort; when she spoke, her voice was so low that I could only just catch the words.

'I have come to beg you not to announce to everyone, at Ruan's coming-of-age ball,

244

that you are his father!'

'You can't cheat me of the pleasure I have waited so long to taste!' he retorted. 'I told you, long ago, that one day I would revenge your rejection of me. You broke the vows we made.'

'That is absurd. We were sixteen years old, hardly more than children.'

'We made vows,' he insisted, eyes narrowed. 'I wanted you, Rose; you and the island. The island was Jerome's, but I promised myself I would get it back from him one day; but you married *him,* a man old enough to be your father! You didn't love *him!*'

I heard the sneer in his voice; but the look on her face as she answered, set her apart from him in a way that nothing else could have done.

'No, I didn't love him, then. It grew slowly, through the years; it began to grow after Ruan was born when I suffered agonies of guilt, seeing Jerome's delight in the child he thought was his son. You know nothing of love and everything of passion.'

'You rejected me; damn you, Rose! You let your father send me away, like a beggar. *You* had money, position, the island that should have been mine—and *my* son. I had—*Irene!*' He laughed derisively.

'You married her for her money and squandered it!' Rose replied evenly.

'Squandered it? No. I made prudent investments with the money I persuaded her to part with, and they have served me well. I may not be able to match Jerome's wealth, but I am, as they say, "comfortably placed". Whereas Irene is almost penniless; a reversal of fortune that causes her some distress.'

'You *are* evil!' she said. 'You've heaped terrible humiliation on Irene!'

'As I will upon Jerome!' he cried triumphantly.

'No, Damien! His heart is not strong. The shock could prove fatal!'

'I told you, the day I arrived here for the celebrations, that I would take the revenge I'd always promised myself!' he retorted.

'What good will it do you? Ruan will hate you!'

'You, too, my dear. Who will hate you most, I wonder—Jerome or Ruan?'

He was supremely arrogant; utterly self-assured. Rose's voice was quiet and controlled.

'Jerome means more to me than anyone

else in the world. There is one way in which I can stop you from making your announcement.'

'Tell me!' he jeered.

'Years ago, my father made me take a solemn oath on his bible. He made me swear that I would never tell a living soul what really happened on the afternoon that Edith died. I have never broken that vow; but I *shall* do so, if you hurt Jerome. I shall make public the fact that *you* killed Edith!'

I thought I had suffered all the shocks my mind could bear. I was wrong; but I felt curiously detached, as though I was watching a play on a stage. Damien Ashley had killed Edith Freemantle...

'Do you imagine anyone will be interested after twenty-five years?' he jeered.

'The authorities will listen with great interest to my tale.'

'And discount it; you have no proof, no witnesses. It will sound like the petty spite of a woman who has been publicly denounced as a whore!'

'They *will* listen,' she replied determinedly. 'I shall *make* them listen to me! You *did* kill her, Damien; you know you did!'

'It was an accident!' he flung at her.

'It was *not!* She came down to the grotto and saw us there, and started shouting that she would tell papa. You pushed her...'

'She was taunting us, just as she taunted Vinnie. You were hysterical! All I wanted to do was get rid of her...'

'You climbed down afterwards, and saw that she was dead, Damien. You told me you were going to get away in your boat, and come back to Easter that evening as though you had been sailing all day. You climbed up and saw poor Vinnie lying on the path, and said we were lucky, that no one would ever know the truth.'

'How well you remember it all! However, your threat is empty, Rose. Even if you are believed, you must produce proof; and you have none.'

I saw, in her face, the realisation that he was right; the tears ran down her cheeks. She looked at him imploringly. It shocked me to see Rose beg for mercy from this man.

'Please don't hurt Jerome!' she pleaded.

'Jerome! *Jerome!*' he cried savagely. 'Do you think I care about *him!* He's had his precious island all these years, but it is *my* son who will inherit it! You told me that you were Mistress of Bella Careena when

I said that you had no right to invite Flora here! Did you plan that she should marry Ruan—to spite me?'

'No!' she replied. 'I did not. To me, Ruan *is* Jerome's son, not yours!'

'I will decide whom Ruan shall marry,' Damien said coolly. 'I shall control his future, on this island.'

'You are mad!' she told him contemptuously. 'Ruan has a will of his own!'

'I am his father!' It was a triumphant hymn, coming from Damien's lips, on the still morning air. 'Irene will go back to London; when Jerome is dead, and Bella has gone away—and *I* shall see to it that she leaves here—then you may stay or go, as you wish. Perhaps I will let you live at Seawinds. Flora, if she chooses, shall live with me at the House of the Four Winds.'

'Oh, God!' she whispered, bowing her head. 'Truly you are mad, Damien!'

'I have waited so long!' he said, softly and yearningly. 'All these years. You thought I had forgotten, didn't you, Rose?'

She stared at him, for a moment; then she turned and walked swiftly along the beach. Her head was still bowed, her bright hair lay like a shawl over her shoulders.

I was jerked sharply back to reality by the realisation that Damien would probably return by the way he had come to the grotto, and find me there.

I scrambled quickly to my feet, the skirt of my dress caught fast on a thorny branch. Frightened, I bent and tugged it free, tearing the material. I left a scrap of the material hanging on the bush, as I began to run, crouching low, not looking back until I came to the place where the path entered the belt of trees.

From the shelter of the trees, I looked back; there was no sign of Damien; however, I didn't slacken speed. I went on, under the green boughs, and across the clearing where the tower stood sentinel. Involuntarily, I glanced upwards, but there was no sign of the sparrowhawk, the bird that waits for the right moment before swooping down silently on its victim.

Head bent, my feet carrying me as fast as my laboured breath would allow, I made for the cottage. It was still very early, and no one was about as I went up to my room. I collapsed on the bed, shivering, sobbing for breath. The morning was still grey and the sun had not risen in the east; it was hidden behind a thick bank of humid cloud.

The golden days had come to an end.

The tears ran down my cheeks. I suddenly hated Rose, I hated Damien, and most of all I hated my own stupidity and the fact that Edwin Trehearne had been right in his assessment of me.

I was composed when Bella Careena came to my room. I had learned in the past hour what Rose had long before learned; that it is possible to contain terrible anguish within oneself and present a calm, unruffled surface to the world.

At breakfast, Nanny Radford said:

'Mr Jardine's had a nasty fall, I hear. Got up early this morning and slipped in his bedroom. Mrs Jardine was there; no bones broken, thank goodness, and he's a bit shook up. Hurt his back. Bruised it, he said, and he won't let Mrs Jardine send for a doctor. Stubborn, that one...'

After breakfast, Bella Careena insisted on going straight to her father. I followed slowly. The air was thick and cloying, and the heavy sky seemed to press down upon me like an iron weight. My hands and face were damp with perspiration, every movement was an effort, and my clothes clung to me most uncomfortably.

Though I knew that I moved and spoke normally, I was still in a state of shock. When I saw Damien standing on the terrace of Four Winds, I could scarcely breathe. I forced myself to walk slowly towards him, to look at him, and wish him good-day.

He smiled charmingly.

'Flora, you don't look yourself,' he said.

'I am very well, thank you.'

'There will be a storm,' he said, looking up at the sky.

He stood as still as one of the statues in the Temple of the Four Winds; only a little wind, blowing in from the sea, lifted the thick gold curls on his forehead.

'I hear that Jerome has met with an accident,' he added.

'Yes. I am going to Rose now,' I told him.

He made no attempt to detain me as I moved past him. I had been hot; now I was so cold that I felt as though I was encased in a sheet of ice. I went upstairs, and met Rose outside Jerome's room.

I asked her how he was.

'He's resting,' she said. 'He wrenched his back, and refuses to have Dr Samuels.

He'll have to stay in bed for a few days.'

I said heavily:

'I want to talk to you, please, Rose.'

'Come to my sitting room,' she said. 'Bella Careena and Ruan are with Jerome. They'll keep him amused for half an hour.'

Half an hour? Was that long enough to tell her how much I despised her for a silence that had lasted twenty-five years and robbed my mother of her good name?

She sat upright on a green velvet chair, hands folded in her lap, and I sat opposite her. I saw the way her fingertips moved restlessly, as though they would not be quiet.

'The air is so still that it seems as though the world has stopped breathing,' she said. 'Flora, something is wrong; what is it?'

'This morning, I followed Damien to the Grotto of the Sun,' I told her flatly. 'I hid behind the bushes to surprise him, and then you came. I heard everything that passed between you. You let my mother be blamed for Edith's death all these years, yet you knew Damien had killed her!'

'Oh, dear God!' she whispered brokenly. 'Oh, Flora, I am sorry!'

253

'*Sorry?*' I said scornfully.

Her head was bent; her fingers plucked at the material of her skirt, and her voice shook.

'You do not know the anguish and guilt I have suffered through the years, Flora,' she whispered. 'If you knew, you would not condemn me. I believed it to be the price I paid for my happiness with my husband. There *were* times when I forgot...'

'*Forgot?* You didn't really care about my mother...!'

'Oh yes, I did, Flora! I have *always* cared, I went straight to my father and told him the truth. He wasn't angry because I had disgraced myself, being found by Edith in a compromising situation with Damien; oh no! He was afraid that if there was any scandal or suspicion attached to Edith's death, he wouldn't get a penny of her money. He said if anyone discovered the truth he would see to it that Damien was charged with murder and spent a lifetime in prison. I was sixteen years old, Flora. I believed him. He made me swear a solemn oath.'

'That oath wasn't binding, under the circumstances!' I retorted scornfully.

'I believed it to be so, Flora.'

'Perhaps you were so infatuated with Damien that you were afraid of what would happen to *him* if the truth was known!' I said bitterly.

She lifted her head and looked at me; there was sorrow, but no anger, in the beautiful blue eyes.

'Yes, I *was* infatuated. Even after I married Jerome at my father's insistence. Until the day, two years after our marriage, when Jerome was away, and Damien came to the island for the first time since it all happened. Three weeks later, when Jerome returned, I knew I was pregnant. If only I had not hurled the truth at Damien then, telling him I never wanted to see him again! Ruan doesn't resemble him, even in features; but he *is* Damien's son, and that has been another burden of guilt that I have carried.'

'You should have told Jerome the whole truth then!' I said.

'It is easy to be wise in maturity. I didn't know what to do! All these years, it has seemed as though Ruan was truly Jerome's son. Damien married Irene, and I believed, then, that the whole unhappy business was ended.'

'Why was Damien on the island the day that Edith died?' I asked.

'He knew we were going for a picnic. My father disapproved of our friendship so we used to meet when we could, in secret. It seemed so wonderful, so exciting, then. Damien sailed his boat to the bay...you heard what he said: we made vows in the chapel, then we went to the cave. I heard Edith coming along singing her silly rhyme about Plain Jane out in the rain...Vinnie hated it... I heard Vinnie shout at her, and Edith was laughing...then Edith came down the path and ran into the grotto... Damien was about to...make love to me, and he was furious with her... It *was* an accident, I suppose...'

She looked piteously at me. All the hate ran out of me. My mother wouldn't have wanted me to feel bitterness towards Rose, who had been a sixteen-year-old girl, trapped like a fly in a spider's web of deceit that had wound its threads more tightly around her through the years. She had been at the mercy of one man's obsession and another man's greed, and had paid dearly for both.

'Did you try to kill Damien?' I asked suddenly.

She looked dumbfounded.

'Never! Why?'

'I was thinking of the arrow shot at us, when we were on the lake; and of the falling statue...but then, you would have *seen* it wasn't Damien, but me, in the temple...oh, I don't understand...'

'If I say that I wish will all my heart and soul that Damien *was* dead, you will think I am wicked, I suppose?'

'Wicked? No, Rose. It's a perfectly natural wish, even if it's morally wrong. You're caught in a trap.'

'Of my own making!' she said, with intense bitterness. 'I would not willingly have forfeited your friendship, Flora.'

'You haven't forfeited it. I don't hate you. Hatred belongs to people like Damien, who feed it...what is to be done, though? If Damien keeps his promise, the shock of knowing the truth will kill Jerome. But will you do as you told him you would, and tell the truth about the day in the Shell Grotto?'

She lifted a weary, tear-streaked face.

'You heard what he said! I have no witnesses, no proof! Oh, Flora, every day the threat that Damien has made comes closer, and every day I pray for a miracle!'

'If Jerome loves you as much as you say he does, then he will forgive you for what happened,' I told her gently.

'He will forgive, Flora; but the damage will have been done and if the shock should prove too great for him, as well it may, of what use will forgiveness be to me?'

I heard the wretchedness of her cry. I went over to her, put my arms around her, and said that there was time yet to find a solution. She didn't believe me, but at least I felt she was comforted a little.

When I went downstairs, Damien was still on the terrace, walking up and down. He looked at me sharply as I stepped out into the air.

'There is thunder in the distance, and I can smell rain,' he said. 'Let us hope the storm blows itself out today and does not spoil tomorrow's festivities.'

'What festivities?' I asked.

'The yearly fair at Easter and Tolfrey. It's quite a big affair. All the servants who can be spared will attend. Ruan is going. The boat will take them over tomorrow morning and bring them back late tomorrow night,' he said.

I turned and almost ran from him.

Halfway across to the cottage, I looked over my shoulder. He was still standing on the terrace, watching me.

The storm broke in all its fury an hour later. In the stillness that preceded the storm I felt a quality of menace about the island; the sleeping cat, curled in the sun, was wide-awake, claws out.

The rain came, pattering heavily through the trees; and then the wind that comes before a storm, making the trees toss their heads wildly, like restive horses. Lightning cut the clouds apart as it flew, jagged and brilliant, from end to end of the sky; the thunder raged above us, and the sea raced angrily inshore, the waves white-capped. Bella Careena enjoyed it. Nanny Radford was frankly terrified.

It lasted for a couple of hours, then the thunder rolled away over the Dorset coast, and the rain stopped; but the sky remained ominously heavy.

I performed several small services for Rose and for Nanny Radford; I stood patiently whilst Miss Hyams fitted my gowns, and all the time an idea was growing, taking shape, become feasible...

I did not want to go to dinner that

evening at the House of the Four Winds, but Rose pleaded with me to put in an appearance.

'I shall be glad of your support, Flora,' she told me wistfully. 'It is becoming daily more difficult to hide what I feel...'

I had three hours before I needed to dress for dinner; it was long enough.

Damien had said scathingly to Rose that her testimony against him would be useless because she had no witnesses and no proof; but my letter to Alexander Arkwright would be a report of facts that I had overheard in the Sun Grotto, and would state, in detail, the admission that Damien had made about Edith's death.

In my letter, I said nothing about Rose's reason for being in the Shell Grotto on the day Edith died, nor did I mention the circumstances surrounding Ruan's conception. I cherished a hope that those facts might never be made public—even though it was a faint hope.

I told Alexander Arkwright that I had discovered my mother's identity, and wished to clear her name, hence the reason for my letter; I instructed him that enquiries and investigations were to be made with all speed, and also informed him that Mr Damien Ashley was not aware that I knew of his part in Edith's death.

My real reason for the letter went much deeper; investigations would mean that Damien would undoubtedly have to leave the island before the coming-of-age celebrations began. Rose would have to back up my evidence, but who would condemn her for keeping silent for so many years after she had sworn, on oath, never to reveal the truth? The fact that she now had to reveal it would undoubtedly only evoke feelings of sympathy. Jerome would be shocked; but the shock would be less than the discovery of his wife's infidelity.

The idea I had mulled over all day seemed to me to be bold and clever; certainly it would take Damien by complete surprise. Let him shout to the world, *afterwards,* that Ruan was his son! The world would look upon it as a desire for revenge, the tables would be neatly and completely turned and disaster might yet be averted; or so I believed.

When at last, I was satisfied with the letter, I folded it, put it in an envelope and sealed it firmly. Tomorrow, I thought, it will be on its way to Bideford.

Chapter 10

I had little appetite for dinner that evening.
There were seven of us: Rose and Edwin,
Damien and Irene, Bella Careena, Ruan
and myself.

We dined indoors; the weather was
cooler, with a wind blowing in from the
sea; lightning still flickered far out across
the water and thunder grumbled in the
distance.

Both Damien and Ruan were attentive
to me, and I managed to maintain
conversation of a light-hearted nature that
didn't tax me too much.

As for Irene, she surprised us all by
her animation. She who was usually so
pale and so quiet, had a feverish gaiety
about her.

'Damien, my dearest, why do you not
join me at the butts more often? With a
little practice, your skill with the arrows
would almost match mine!' she said gaily.

'I have no desire to match your skill at
archery, my dear Irene,' Damien retorted

smoothly. 'I prefer a gun.'

'Ah yes!' she murmured. 'The flight of a bullet or the flight of an arrow—what is the difference, if the target is the same? The purpose of both is to kill.'

'Not on this island!' Rose said firmly.

'So we practise for a killing we shall never make. A sad waste of talent, I think,' Irene replied.

'Whom do you wish to kill?' Edwin asked her, with interest.

Her eyes were wide, brilliant, and unfocussed.

'Why, no one, Edwin. I merely say it is a waste of talent if weapons are not used for the purpose for which they were intended!' she replied.

'Did you kill the peacock?' Bella Careena asked bluntly.

There was dead silence. Rose looked reprovingly at her daughter, Ruan was aghast.

'Yes,' Irene replied. 'I killed it.'

The silence was electric. I saw the look on the faces of the two servants who were waiting with the serving dishes; Irene seemed to enjoy the attention she was causing.

'I was going to Seawinds,' she said

gaily. 'As I came near Laurie's forge, I remembered you and Miss Lindsay were going to spend an afternoon on the lake, Damien. I was going to ask Laurie for an arrow and bow, but he wasn't there, so I took them. I saw you getting out of the boat with Miss Lindsay, and I wanted to frighten you. No, that isn't true; I wanted to kill *you*, Damien. After all, you have many times wished *me* dead, and stated so; is that not true?'

The silence was terrifying; I could hear the drumbeats of my heart in my own ears.

Rose made a valiant attempt to retrieve the situation; she looked appalled.

'Irene, you must not say such things! You are ill...'

'*Ill?*' Irene shook her head, laughing. 'No, I am not, Rose. I am *well!*' She turned to me, and gave me a smile of unearthly brilliance. 'Dear Miss Lindsay, you have no *idea* what a narrow escape you had on the night of the party. You were waiting in the Temple of the Four Winds for my husband, were you not?'

'No!' I whispered, furious and horrified.

'Ah, but you *were!* The temptation was not to be resisted. To kill you or to frighten

265

you...it made no difference... Have I not said before that you would be surprised at the strength in these wrists and arms, Miss Lindsay? I am not soft and weak as Damien would like to think!'

Edwin sprang to his feet with such speed that he overturned his glass of wine. The glass shattered and a stain spread across the white cloth.

'Flora could have been killed!' he said, his face white with anger.

'Exactly what I have said, my dear Edwin...'

With immense dignity, Rose stood up.

'Irene, you *are* ill; much more ill than you realise. You must return to Seawinds and go to bed...you need to be properly cared for...'

Irene shook her head, smiling; her smile had a vague quality, and I felt chilled. Damien's face was like granite. He stood up, and said curtly:

'Come, Irene.'

Irene rose to her feet; she shook off Damien's arm, smiled again, wished us all goodnight, and informed her husband that she was quite capable of making her own way back to Seawinds.

However, Damien insisted upon accompanying her. The carriage was brought to the door, and one of the servants was sent to the farm for Mrs Clegg. Rose instructed two maids to clear away the rest of the meal. No one had any appetite.

It was a silent party that gathered in the drawing-room. Coffee was served to us, and the servants left us alone. Only then did Rose speak.

'Poor Irene!' she whispered. 'How dreadful. Oh, how *dreadful!*'

'A mental breakdown,' Edwin said shortly. 'Caused by Damien's treatment of her, I imagine.'

'It's the curse of the peacocks,' Bella Careena declared.

'Oh, Bella, that's stupid nonsense!' Rose cried sharply.

Edwin stood up and said calmly:

'It has been a distressing evening. I suggest that an early night would be of benefit to us all.'

Rose nodded, relief in her face.

'The boat will leave at eight o'clock tomorrow morning,' she said. 'As you are going to Dorchester on business, Edwin, you may like to take the early boat. It will cross again at noon, with the rest of the servants who are going to the fair.'

'Will the mail go out as usual, at four o'clock?' I asked.

'Not tomorrow. It will go at eight—and again at noon.'

'I have a letter,' I said. 'I should like it to be on its way as soon as possible.'

'Then have it here by half-past seven for Hawkins to put in his satchel,' Rose told me.

I had a restless night. The thought that Irene had tried to kill me was so incredible that I found it difficult to believe. But I knew that Edwin was right. Damien, by his treatment of his wife, had lit a fire that had smouldered on and finally burst into flame.

I was up and dressed by seven o'clock next morning. It was raining hard and the skies were pewter-coloured. I felt sorry for the servants who were going to the fair. They had all looked forward to the outing; and only the older ones, like Nanny Radford, did not want to go.

I put on a cloak and turned up the hood; with my precious letter hidden under the cloak, I stepped out into the rain that was driving in relentlessly from the sea.

I did not expect to see Damien; but he

was there, sheltering under the trees just beyond the house; I stared apprehensively at him; but there was nothing in his face to alarm me as he came up to me and said:

'I'm on my way to Clegg's farm; Mrs Clegg was good enough to spend the best part of the night with Irene.'

'How is Irene?' I asked, staring straight ahead, as I walked swiftly towards the house.

'Sleeping soundly. Mrs Clegg gave her a sedative. Irene's behaviour has been odd recently, and I have heard something like this might happen.'

I did not answer him; I hated him and had no desire to talk to him.

He insisted on coming to the house with me. My hands were shaking as I took the letter from my cloak and thrust it hastily into the big leather satchel lying on the table. I felt cold sweat break out along my forehead; Damien was standing in the hall talking to Hawkins.

By ten o'clock, it had stopped raining, though the skies remained heavy and there was a strong sea running.

Dr Samuels came over when the boat returned from its eight o'clock trip, and

269

went straight to Seawinds.

Later I saw Rose; she told me that Dr Samuels had called on her after his visit to Seawinds, and had stated that Mrs Ashley seemed quite rational and had apologised profusely for her behaviour of the previous evening, saying that she had drunk a great deal of wine before coming to the House of the Four Winds.

I stared at Rose.

'It isn't true,' I said.

'No, it isn't. Dr Samuels seemed convinced, though. I believe he thought we were making a great fuss about nothing.' She looked uneasily at me. 'I repeated what Irene had said. He laughed and told me it was a highly dramatic piece of fantasy for which, undoubtedly, an excess of wine was responsible.'

Irene was being very cunning. I didn't like it. I wished the day was over, that Ruan and Edwin were back on the island. I felt isolated, and it was not a pleasant feeling...

Dr Samuels had left a supply of powders which were to be given to Irene if she became over-excited. He declined Rose's offer of lunch, and went back to the mainland at noon with the rest of the island servants.

Jerome was still confined to his bed. Dr Samuels had seen him and advised a further period of rest. Rose, Bella Careena and I had lunch together, and we were a silent trio; even Bella Careena seemed to have lost her usual good spirits. No one had seen Damien since he had come to the house with me, early that morning.

The wind rose after lunch, it blew in sharp, squally gusts that gradually reached gale force as the tide turned and began to race in, breaking into great plumes of foam all along the shore.

At five o'clock, Rose said grimly:

'If this weather continues, the boat won't be able to come back this evening.'

I felt a terrible sense of loneliness. I wanted the boat to come back. I wanted Edwin, who had said 'I love you' to a woman who hadn't listened...

'What will they do?' I asked.

'Oh, they'll stay at the Fortune, quite comfortably,' she told me.

The violence of the storm was terrifying. I thought it would lift the house and carry it bodily away. Bella Careena listened to the noise of the gale howling outside with a dreamy look on her face.

'The bells of Lost Atlantis are ringing under the sea,' she said.

'It's a pretty story, but I'm in no mood for your fancies,' I told her wryly.

'You're safe here,' she assured me. 'Quite safe.'

It was an evening on which the darkness would come early; the clouds were very low in the sky, racing in with the swollen seas.

After tea Bella Careena went upstairs to play chess with her father.

'I'll go back to the cottage,' I told Rose. 'Nanny Radford doesn't like being left on her own, especially when the weather is bad.'

Nanny was pleased to see me; she had lit a fire in her small sitting room, and was huddled over it, declaring that she had caught a cold and no wonder, the way the weather changed.

At seven o'clock, she went to bed; I looked out of the window at the lights burning in the House of the Four Winds, and wondered how long it would be before Bella Careena returned. The wind seemed to have dropped a little, I reflected thankfully. Perhaps the boat would get back.

When I heard the knock at the door, some time later, my heart missed a beat; Bella Careena would not have knocked... I opened the door.

Damien stood there; for a moment, I thought I was going to suffocate. This man, so tall, so handsome, had sent a child to her death, and held a woman to ransom for her folly...and a little while ago I had believed I loved him with all my heart.

'What is it?' I asked.

There was not a vestige of a smile on his face; he stared sombrely at me.

'It's Irene,' he said. 'She's very ill. I gave her a sedative this afternoon, but it seems to have had no effect. She's in a fever and delirious. There are only two elderly servants in the house, so I'm going to Clegg's farm for Lucy. Will you go to Seawinds, Flora? I can scarcely ask Rose.'

I looked at him suspiciously. I didn't trust him; but what harm could come to me, with two servants and Lucy Clegg in the house? Who else was there? At Four Winds there was only an elderly man, sick and confined to his bed, a girl of fourteen—and Rose. The island was shorn of its usual staff; Ruan and Edwin were away.

Nevertheless, I felt distinctly uneasy.

'It's a long walk in this weather, even if I take the short cuts,' I told him.

'Then wait here until I return with Lucy Clegg,' he said shortly. 'Though I would prefer that you went straight to Irene. I am desperately worried about her, in view of what happened last night.'

He turned and strode away, towards Clegg's farm.

I fetched my cloak; I listened at Nanny's door; she was sound asleep. I scribbled a note for Bella Careena, telling her where I had gone, and let myself out of the cottage.

There was still plenty of daylight left; I hated walking under the trees, for it was dark there, but I made my way as fast as I could in the direction of Seawinds, remembering all the short cuts that Bella Careena had showed me.

I avoided looking at the ruined chapel; from there it was a short walk to the wide path that led to the Shell Grotto. I had to cross the path, pass under a short tunnel of trees, and then I would come out at the back of Seawinds.

He was waiting for me; at the end of the tunnel. He stepped into my path and his arms went around me like a vice. I screamed again and again, but the sound was borne away on the wind, and, somewhere, a peacock screamed in answer.

He hadn't been near Clegg's farm! He had come back here, to wait for me!

I struggled fiercely against him; he held me closer, laughing. In the tunnel of trees, no one could see us.

'Why?' I panted furiously. '*Why*, Damien?'

'Because you are dangerous, Flora Lindsay. You wrote a letter, a very damning letter. I've read it with interest; and destroyed it. I've spent a lot of time watching you, Flora, ever since you were at the Sun Grotto.'

So he had seen me; he knew that I had all the information I needed to condemn him. My heart sank like a stone to the bottom of the pool.

'You weren't quick or clever enough!' he said contemptuously. 'I saw you running away; I found a piece of material on the bushes, torn from your dress. I asked Bella Careena what you did yesterday after tea. She said you were busy writing a letter.

That interested me; so I watched again this morning, and saw how anxious you were to hide your letter away in the safety of the satchel that Hawkins took to the jetty. There was very little in the satchel, when I examined it—which I did, the moment you had left the house.'

I had failed; the bitterness of failure ousted every other feeling for a moment. Damien had won, he would create havoc worse than anything the storm could bring.

'Curiosity is a fine servant and a bad master, Flora,' he told me. 'It served me well, you must agree!'

'You can't keep *me* silent!' I cried defiantly. 'I know the truth! I shall tell it...'

'No. You will be dead by the time they start looking for you,' he said calmly.

Horror filled me, and a frantic desire to escape from that vice-like grip, to run and run...

He only held me tighter; his voice was almost playful.

'On such a night, who will be surprised that there is a casualty of the storm?'

I bent my head back as far as it would go, glaring at him.

'I left a note for Bella Careena, telling

her I was going to Seawinds,' I told him.

'It will be some time, yet, before she finds it. It won't unduly alarm her, for she will think you are at Seawinds. When they come looking for you, *I* shall be there, with Irene whom I have not left unattended. Who can disprove my story? In years to come, Bella Careena will spin another pretty tale to prove that the island is cursed; and you, Flora, will be *dead!*'

He turned me round with such violence that I almost over-balanced and pinned my arms behind my back in an agonisingly painful grip until tears ran down my cheeks. He thrust me in front of him, forcing me to walk back along the tunnel to the path that led to the Shell Grotto.

'Vinnie's daughter!' he cried. 'What a fitting end for the daughter of the governess! I would have made you my mistress! We should both have enjoyed that; but your curiosity will sign your death-warrant!'

I knew what he intended to do, for he was forcing me to stumble in front of him along the path leading to the Shell Grotto; the path my mother had once walked, looking for Edith. I heard the hiss of waves below us.

'Will you kill a second time?' I cried bitterly.

'Yes! With so much within my grasp, do you suppose I shall let you cheat me of victory? When you are dead, only Rose will know what happened to Edith, and her testimony is worth *nothing!*'

I sent up a last fierce, desperate prayer. I never really believed, until then, that prayers are sometimes answered.

'Damien!' The voice was high, clear and commanding.

He had the presence of mind to spin me round with him, as he turned.

I saw her standing on the path, smiling; a small woman, neatly dressed, the hood of a cloak almost covering her fawn-coloured hair. She wore a quiver of arrows that gave her a medieval look, as though she had stepped from an old painting. She carried a bow, to which she was carefully fitting an arrow.

'Irene!' he shouted angrily. 'You are ill...I left you sleeping...'

'So you thought, my dear Damien. I decided that tonight would be a good time for a peacock hunt.'

'A *peacock hunt!'* he said, astounded.

'Yes. I have six arrows. Laurie has gone

to the fair...he wasn't at the forge when I went there a little while ago, so I took a stone and broke his window. I wanted the bow and some arrows for the hunt. I shall hunt the peacock; a beautiful bird, vain, arrogant. I shall bring him down, in all his pride and beauty, and see his plumage trail in the dust.'

She spoke quite calmly; but in the dying light, I could see the glitter of her eyes.

I heard Damien laugh.

'If you shoot that arrow, my dear Irene, it will kill *Flora!*'

'Very well. I shall kill the peahen first,' she retorted. 'Your mistress—and then *you!*'

'I am *not* his mistress!' I cried furiously.

'Yes, you are, Flora. *You* are the reason he intends to stay here instead of returning to London with me. I have suffered years of humiliation and tonight it will be at an end; my aim will be the better for my memories!'

Damien held me in a powerful grip from which I could not free myself; standing there, only a few yards from Irene, I was a certain target.

I tried to duck; from somewhere, I found a strength I did not know I possessed.

279

My arms were almost wrenched from the sockets, and I screamed at the top of my voice. The sound put Irene off her stroke for an instant, and it gave me fresh heart; frantically, I wriggled from side to side, trying to free myself, and the fury of my movements caused Damien to shift his position.

The arrow was ready; Irene had only to release it from the bow. I thrust myself forward as far as I could, at the same time kicking backwards through clinging skirts. It was a superhuman effort.

It worked; I went to the ground, and Damien came down on top of me, cursing furiously. He was a heavy man, and I was winded completely for a few seconds; but I rolled away, bruised, grazed, muddied from the wet, slippery ground—but alive.

Damien got to his feet; the arrow whistled past his head, just missing him. He crouched low, ready to make a lunge at Irene, as she fitted the second arrow. He measured the distance between them and then hurled himself at her.

He missed her by a fraction of an inch, though she dropped the arrow. She let it lie where it fell; she took another and, instead of fitting it to the bow, held it in her hand,

and lifted it above her head like a spear.

I felt sick; I hated Damien, but I had no wish to see him killed. I saw the deadly purpose in her face; the horror in his, as he clawed at her skirts, trying to pull her down; but she remained just out of reach, arrow poised, waiting.

The moment seemed like eternity. Damien suddenly lost his nerve. He rolled away from her along the path, then scrambled wildly to his feet and backed away; I believe he suddenly thought of the Shell Grotto, knowing that if he could reach it he would have the advantage of Irene; he crouched low, running towards the top of the path; the second arrow sped from the bow as he reached the top and began to scramble down.

For the second time it just missed him; but it unnerved him. The rain had made the path slippery, haste and fear made him clumsy. He slipped; floundered, and regained his balance; slipped again and hurtled headlong down to the beach where waves hissed and foamed over the rocks.

I closed my eyes against the whirling kaleidoscope of sand, sea and sky. I saw Irene walk to the end of the path and look down with an air of detachment. I thought of the sea clawing at Damien, carrying him away. I thought of the eyes of the mermaid and the sea-serpent; ice-cold, like Irene's; glittering, like Irene's as she turned to me, and smiled.

'I have four arrows left,' she said. 'I shall not waste them, Flora! The sea has taken the peacock; now for its mate!'

Irene was mad. Stiffly I scrambled to my feet. I was taller than she was, but I doubted that I had her strength. She picked up her bow; went back and picked up the arrow she had dropped, whilst I thought furiously.

'If you are going to hunt me,' I said, 'then you must give me at least a few minutes start. Those are the rules; where is the sport in taking a sitting target? You have to *prove* your skill...'

She looked at me thoughtfully, head on one side; then she laughed happily.

'Don't be silly, my dear Miss Lindsay. You must think I am mad to be taken in by such a suggestion. If you have a few *minutes* you will easily elude me and that would never do. I will give you ten seconds...'

I turned and ran as though the Devil himself was at my heels. I was running level with the cliffs and the beach, but I had turned westwards, not eastwards. I was heading for the westernmost tip of the island, a place to which I had never been.

Inevitably, I came to the trees again; the blessed, friendly trees, growing thickly together in a small plantation of firs that hid me from Irene's eyes. An arrow sang past me, and was lost in the green gloom; she was finding it more difficult to aim at a moving target in a poor light than to send her arrows at a fixed target on a sunny afternoon.

She had three arrows left; if I could elude them until daylight ran out, then I would be safe.

The trees began to thin; I avoided using the little paths, because it was safer to keep away from them; nevertheless, the next arrow barely missed my head, and, during a lull in the wind, I heard Irene's laughter.

Two arrows left; no more trees to shelter me. I was on open ground, running up a rise, with Seawinds away on my right. I thought of trying to make a detour to the house, and decided against it; she would trap me there.

I reached the top of the rise, went over it and collapsed, sobbing, into a small grassy depression on the other side. My breath cut painfully through my lungs; I lifted my head cautiously, and saw Irene standing where the trees ended—waiting.

Hopelessly, I looked around me. The slope descended gently to open turf, with no paths and only a few stunted bushes. The land was so narrow here that I could see the water on either side of me, and, ahead of me, white spray broke over a low headland.

Directly in front of me, on the tip of the island, only a few yards from the headland, was what seemed to be a long, low stone building.

Irene was still waiting at the edge of the trees. There was no way back for me, and she knew it. Ahead was the unfriendly sea. Seawinds was behind me, away to my right, and I could never reach it unseen.

There might be somewhere to hide in the stone building. I slithered down the slope and raced towards it, wondering why it had no doors or windows; when I finally reached it, I discovered that it was a tomb, similar to Ann Churnock's. There was a name carved on it that I could not read.

The turf was uneven, there appeared to have been a small landslide, disturbing the ground and damaging the landward end of the tomb, for there was a gaping hole, bricks spilled everywhere, and a thick wooden door hanging from its hinges. It occurred to me, fleetingly, that it could not be a very old tomb if it was built of bricks.

If I stayed in there until it was quite dark, I could then make my way back across the island to Four Winds, I thought, as I crawled into the hole. I could taste the salt spray on my lips; the waves were very near, but at least they wouldn't come this far.

I don't know what I expected to find inside; certainly not a flight of steps, down which I hurtled to a stone floor.

I lay there stunned; there were two oblongs of greyish light in the wall above me, and the sea sounded very loud. I could see nothing else in the thick gloom.

I was very battered and bruised, exhausted and aching in every limb, but at least I was safe for a while. It was a comforting thought to take me down into the soft darkness that lapped around me...

I drifted hazily between consciousness and unconsciousness; when I finally roused myself with a supreme effort, it was pitch dark.

I put out my hand and found smooth stone. I rose unsteadily to my feet and carefully felt my way around the wall. The inside of the tomb seemed much bigger than one would imagine from the outside.

I steeled myself against finding some grisly remains; I moved slowly, keeping against the wall, feeling with my hands, until I came to the place where I had seen the oblongs of greyish light; they were still there, faint relief from the deep gloom around me.

I put up my hands; to my astonishment, my fingertips felt glass, thick and smooth. I went on probing with my fingers until I found what I thought was a catch. When I tugged it, the glass slid back, the sea sounded as though it was all around me and the night air whistled more coldly than ever.

Beyond the glass, my hands encountered iron bars. I could see the white caps of waves and a few faint stars above them.

The oblongs were two gratings, made

to admit light and air, protected by reinforced glass. I was glad enough to close them, for reaction had set in and I was shivering. I still couldn't see my surroundings; cautiously I put my hands in front of me, sweeping imaginary half circles as I shuffled forward.

I almost bumped into a low table, with a book on it. The table seemed to be carved; beside it, there was a carved stool. I made another much more exciting find; a stone ledge on which I could feel the outline of a lamp. Beside the lamp, I discovered a couple of tapers and a box of matches.

I almost wept with relief...if there was oil in the lamp...!

I wasted half a dozen matches. I crouched, trying to shield the fragile flame from the draught coming down the steps, and I thought I should never get the taper alight. Then, when I finally had the lighted taper in my hand, I had to lift the glass chimney and turn up the wick. My fingers shook so much that I could scarcely hold the taper to the wick; and after I had lit the lamp I had to replace the glass chimney before the flame dipped and went out.

I made it! I had the flame safely sheltered

in its glass prison, and I turned up the wick as far as it would go.

I lifted the lamp high and looked around me. I was in a large stone chamber, roughly circular. There were paintings on the walls; murals of fish and sea-animals, mermaids and dolphins, strange seaweed forests, all done in brilliant colours. There was a map of the island stuck on the wall, and made entirely of small shells. On one wall was written: 'The Grotto of Atlantis'.

This was the fifth grotto. Bella Careena's secret place. I drew a deep breath of pure pleasure, forgetting that I was tired and muddied, and that my arms ached intolerably.

I went across to the table and looked at the book. It was composed of several sheets of thick paper fastened between two covers of carved wood. I lifted the top cover and read aloud from the fly-leaf.

'A history of Bella Careena, by Marcus Trehearne.'

It began with the tale of the first invaders, centuries ago, who had found a floating forest, once part of the mainland, and had thought it was Paradise...

It had been written by hand in beautiful

copper-plate, a long and detailed history; I turned the pages at random. There was a painting of Ann Churnock, with bells sewn to her dress, and a flat basket full of grain on her arm; birds and animals bordered the page. There was an account of Alfrec de Bressard's exploits that made me shiver, an account of the quarrel between the Selwyns; a history that went right up to the day that Caspar Jardine had bought the island from Sylvester Ashley.

Finally, I found the poem at the end of the book. Marcus Trehearne had written it.

LEGEND

Lost Atlantis whispers
In a foam of bells, ice-cold and clear,
From towers of amethyst,
Beneath unfathomed seas.
Along broken streets of pearl
Lonely echoes linger,
And in sleeping gardens, no leaf
Stirs on sunken tree, nor breeze
Ruffles smooth ribbon of fronded weed.
To silken melody
Her shattered cities of turquoise
And coral, gleam iridescent

In slender twist and curl of spire
Undulating through shadowed deep
Her courtyards are dim
With the hush of centuries,
And old palaces of emerald and jade,
Receive again their Kings;
Around her singing fountains,
Full-skirted dancers
Sway like clustered sea-anemones.

Sea-mist winds a silver shroud,
On silent valleys and hills;
From secret harbours, ghostly ships
Ride out across the seas,
To amber cities of the sun,
And rainbow worlds of fantasy.

Lost Atlantis lies
In a vault of emerald, shrouded
In jewels for the splendour
Of her story; remembered
Only where these echoes linger, lonely
On the evening air,
Bells, ice-cold and clear,
Ringing down the centuries,
From the towers of amethyst.

I have never forgotten that night when
I stood in the Grotto of Atlantis, reading

Marcus Trehearne's poems, whilst outside the sea sang to itself in the darkness and the wind grumbled away in the distance.

I closed the book. I came out of yesterday back to the present, and the sudden realisation that the lamplight might give me away to Irene, if she was still watching and waiting, somewhere.

I was confused; I couldn't imagine how long I had been in the grotto though it seemed to have been hours. I turned the wick of the lamp down low, and, with the words of the poem still in my mind, went cautiously up the short flight of stone steps to peer through the gap.

Seawinds seemed to be ablaze with lights; far more than I had seen when I ran from the sheltering trees. Though the sea was still wild, the night was calmer; but I doubted very much if the boat had come back from the mainland.

I sat on the top step, wondering what to do; I was deathly tired; the comfort of a soft bed and hours of dreamless sleep seemed the most precious thing in the world.

When at last I saw lights that moved, I thought it was an illusion; they danced up and down, goblin lights in the night, and as they came nearer, I panicked, remembering Irene...until I heard the voices.

'Flora...Flora...!'

Voices? Ah, there was but one voice!

I stood up.

'Edwin!' I cried. 'Oh, *Edwin!*'

When he reached me, yards ahead of the others, the reaction was so great that I burst into tears. I could not stop, even when he put down his lantern and held me in his arms, rocking me back and forth like a baby.

'Hush...Flora, dearest, hush...you are safe...'

My face was against his shoulder; his arms were strong and gentle. I felt his chin against the top of my head.

'Irene...' I whispered.

'It's all right, Flora. We're going to get you home, now. I thought we'd never find you. There's a boatman in Tolfrey who deserves a medal. He brought Ruan and I over in his boat, and it's not a journey I want to repeat in a hurry. I was worried, so desperately worried about you, though I don't know *why...*'

'I've got something to show you,' I said.

I had to wait whilst he sent Ruan and the

rest of the search party back to Seawinds for a horse and trap; then I took his hand and led him down into the grotto.

Mine was the sheer joy of seeing the wonder in his face, as he looked at the paintings on the walls and read the poem in the book.

'This is the treasure I've looked for,' he told me. 'My father told me before he died that the fifth grotto was his greatest achievement; and you have found it for me...'

I leaned my head against his shoulder.

'I am so glad. Edwin...it's for—Perdita.'

'What is?' he asked, puzzled.

'The "P" on the hairbrush...it's from Shakespeare and it means the lost one.'

There was a long silence; very gently, he kissed my forehead. Then he said:

'I don't think you're lost now, though, are you?'

'No, Edwin; but I am very, very tired. Everything else must wait until tomorrow...'

I don't remember much about the journey back to the House of the Four Winds. I remember that Rose was there, and Bella Careena... I remember brandy that burnt

293

my throat, someone washing away the mud from my face and hands, cool fingers tending the bruises and scratches...then a soft bed and sleep, deep, dreamless...

When I awoke, the sun was shining; the clouds had gone and the sky looked as though it had been rinsed and hung out to dry; the wind was no more than a skittish breeze in the treetops.

Rose was sitting by the window, cheek resting on her hand. She looked very tired; when I spoke her name, she turned her head and came across to sit on the bed. I realised she had been crying.

'Jerome?' I asked fearfully.

'Sleeping. What happened last night was a great shock, but he has taken it well.'

'Irene?' I whispered.

'She is very ill; in a coma. They found her hiding in the Shell Grotto...she said she was waiting for Damien...'

I saw the horror in Rose's eyes; the Shell Grotto; truly it was cursed, I thought.

Rose added: 'It's been such a nightmare. Bella Careena stayed late playing chess with her father, and then suddenly Edwin and Ruan and a few of the menservants arrived...I was so surprised, especially when Edwin said he had been worried about you. We went to the cottage and found your note; then Edwin and Ruan went straight to Seawinds. The two servants there had barricaded themselves in their rooms, frightened because Irene had behaved so strangely, saying she was going to hunt peacocks. They said she wasn't sane...we didn't know what had happened to *you*, and Edwin said he was going to tear the island apart to find you...'

I told her what had happened; I began with the letter and the trap Damien had set.

'How strange life is,' she said, shaking her head. 'You wrote that letter, hoping to make things easier for me...*you*, Vinnie's daughter; and I let Vinnie be blamed all these years...'

'Don't talk about it, Rose. I did it for Jerome, too—because you two have so much love for each other, and it's a rare thing, love like that...'

'There will be investigations,' she said tiredly. 'The police will come.'

'Of course; after that, it will all be over. Whatever you have felt, through the years—remorse, guilt, regret—will be done with, forever.'

'How young you are to be so old and wise!' she said.

Bella Careena came to me later that morning.

'So you found my secret grotto, Flora?'

'By accident. It was a refuge. It may have saved my life. I didn't even know the tomb was there, until last night.'

'It isn't a real tomb,' she told me. 'It's got Alfrec de Bressard's name carved on it, and it says in the book that there was a real tomb, once, but it was washed into the sea. It's a vault made out of rock, and there are two gratings; I found the slits, high up in the rock face above the beach. Then I looked at the brick tomb, the one the Selwyns put there, after the old one was washed away, and I thought: there must be a way in. It was easy!' she said, with a superior air. 'I found a big bunch of keys hanging on a nail in the church porch and one of them fitted the door. *Anyone* could have found it; but no one ever goes to that part of the island. It's like the Shell Grotto: haunted.'

'Oh, Bella Careena...!' I began; but she frowned.

'You shouldn't laugh at me, Flora. Some

296

places are haunted on this island: the Shell Grotto, the ruined chapel; Alfrec's tomb. So I bet Edwin's father thought *that* was a safe place to make the fifth grotto. It's my favourite of them all.'

'Mine too,' I said.

'You wouldn't have got in if the storm hadn't made a bit of a landslide near there,' she pointed out. 'Wasn't Edwin's father clever? The men who went there weren't really workmen at all, they were artists; the Grotto was already made, of course. It's all in the book. I suppose you didn't read it?'

'Some of it; I read the poem,' I sighed. 'Edwin saw it all.'

'*I* wouldn't have told him where it was,' she said calmly. 'People have to find places like that for themselves...'

During the next few days, it seemed that there were strange men everywhere on the island. Men in plain clothes, men in uniform, asking questions. I answered them truthfully, without telling them that Damien had trapped me, nor did I mention the letter. I merely said he had asked me to go to Seawinds because he was worried about Irene...

297

So I kept back some small part of the truth, and I do not regret my silence. The truth would not have helped Damien, whose body was washed up some weeks later along the Hampshire coast; nor would it have helped Irene, who never came out of her coma.

Dr Samuels told the police that he had been sent for on account of Irene's strange behaviour; and the statement of the servants at Seawinds bore out his testimony. Poor Irene! I felt great pity for her. Life had treated her unkindly, and given her little cause for happiness.

Rose insisted on telling Edwin the whole story from beginning to end; so only he and I share her secret, and Ruan and Bella Careena will never know it, thank Heavens.

On the night he asked me to marry him, I told Edwin the truth about my inheritance; he laughed, kissed me, and made a characteristic reply.

'I don't want one penny of your money, my love. Do what you please with it. You can use it to spread happiness where there has been misery, ease the burden of poverty; educate; improve the lot of others. Money is a great treasure, you'll find!'

Epilogue

Jerome Jardine lived for nearly three years after that summer. When he died, Rose told me that they had been the happiest years of her life, years of perfect tranquillity and peace of mind, and the joy in one another that only two people deeply in love can know. Even now, six years after his death, some of that happiness remains with her.

Bella Careena left the island when her father died.

'It is time for me to go,' she told me. 'Ruan is going to travel. I don't think he'll settle in the island, even when he marries. Mama doesn't want to stay any longer, of course. Alfrec de Bressard's tomb has been bricked up, and the grotto will be secret for ever now, though I'm giving Edwin his father's book. It is time for me to see the rest of the world, but I shall always know that the island was mine, more than anyone else's, that I am part of it in a way I can never explain.'

Bella Careena and her mother have travelled far and wide since then and they write to us of strange and wonderful cities, half way across the world. Ruan is married and living at the other end of England.

I hope some day that Bella Careena will fall in love and marry, though she may never go back to the island. I hope she will be as happy as Edwin and I are, today, living quietly in Gloucestershire with our twin sons and baby daughter.

Perhaps none of us will ever return; Edwin says it is better that we should not do so; but I think of the island often, when I am lying awake at night.

The servants have all gone from Bella Careena; there is no one there now, except a caretaker and his wife, and a couple of gamekeepers. I think of the wind walking in the trees. I think of the inscription on Ann Churnock's tomb; *Now will I make fast this day my heart unto yours.* Edwin has had those words engraved on a locket for me.

I think of the Shell Grotto, and the figures with their eyes of glass; of the secret and lovely Grotto of Atlantis, the peacocks strutting everywhere, uttering their weird, unearthly cries, spreading out their exquisite feathers.

I think of these things; then I sigh and turn restlessly, until Edwin, knowing what I am thinking, takes me in his arms, tells me that only today and tomorrow are important, not yesterday.

I know he is right; but my memories live with me still, especially on nights when the wind that blows over our quiet fields seems to smell of the sea.

The publishers hope that this book has given you enjoyable reading. Large Print Books are especially designed to be as easy to see and hold as possible. If you wish a complete list of our books, please ask at your local library or write directly to: Dales Large Print Books, Long Preston, North Yorkshire, BD23 4ND, England.

This Large Print Book for the Partially sighted, who cannot read normal print, is published under the auspices of

THE ULVERSCROFT FOUNDATION